"I know all abou ☞ Y0-BDR-527 think getting a woman into bed should be an Olympic sport."

"I've never said that."

"There's no need to—your actions speak loudly enough."

"You shouldn't believe everything you read."

"Or everything you hear." She folded her arms, wanting to look unmoved, although she was feeling so many emotions she could hardly keep still. "Why did you ~~DISCARD~~

"I wanted to make you stop crying."

Hannah paused, hating how he was a constant surprise to her. "I don't believe you."

He shrugged. "It's the truth. Did the contractor give you a good estimate?"

"No."

"Oh. Look, a friend owes me a favor. I can get your parents' house fixed so they'll get insured."

Hannah held up her hand and shook her head. "I don't need your help—you're the one who needs mine."

Amal shrugged and leaned against her desk. "I don't see why you're so upset. It was a harmless diversion." He continued before she could reply. "Did I try to get your number or address?"

"No."

He folded his arms. "You're lucky I didn't have to resort to Plan B."

"Plan B?"

"Yes." He came around the desk and lifted her to her feet. "I was going to kiss you." And then he did just that. She expected to be repelled, alarmed, violated, but instead the touch of his lips on hers was like coming home. Like the sweet smell of cinnamon pancakes on a Sunday morning, or the sound of a crackling fire on a still winter's night. He felt safe, secure, right.

Books by Dara Girard

Harlequin Kimani Romance

Sparks
The Glass Slipper Project
Taming Mariella
Power Play
A Gentleman's Offer
Body Chemistry
Round the Clock
Words of Seduction
Pages of Passion
Beneath the Covers
All I Want Is You
Secret Paradise
A Reluctant Hero
Perfect Match

DARA GIRARD

fell in love with storytelling at an early age. Her romance-writing career happened by chance when she discovered the power of a happy ending. She is an award-winning author whose novels are known for their sense of humor, interesting plot twists and witty dialogue. When she's not writing, she enjoys spring mornings and autumn afternoons, French pastries, dancing to the latest hits and long drives.

Dara loves to hear from her readers. You can reach her at contactdara@daragirard.com or P.O. Box 10345, Silver Spring, MD 20914.

Perfect Match

DARA GIRARD

HARLEQUIN® KIMANI™ ROMANCE

Recycling programs
for this product may
not exist in your area.

ISBN-13: 978-0-373-86314-3

PERFECT MATCH

HARLEQUIN®

™ www.Harlequin.com

Printed in U.S.A.

Dear Reader,

Have you ever had to work with someone you couldn't stand? That's the situation Hannah finds herself in when she's forced to take on playboy Amal Harper as a client in order to save her parents' home.

I really enjoyed working with the premise of dealing with people who aggravate you. I once had a boss who kept calling me by the wrong name and another who just referred to me as "the girl." Those personalities really helped me develop Mrs. Martha Walker, the one person who, unwittingly, unites Hannah and Amal.

And then of course there's the secret Mrs. Walker is desperate to keep that Hannah is just as determined to uncover.

Soon both women will learn that Amal Harper is not all that he seems and hearts will be broken and healed....

Enjoy,

Dara Girard

Chapter 1

"We're going to be homeless."

"No, you're not."

"We're going to be tossed out in the street and left to starve."

Hannah Olaniyi bit back a sigh as she switched her cell phone to her other ear. Her older sister, Abigail, always tended toward the dramatic. In the distance she heard children squealing with delight as they raced about the playground. A few feet away a jogger darted past and a dog tugged on its leash while attempting to sniff the trunk of a tree. She felt the warmth of the late-spring sun as she strolled through the park on her lunch break. She saw its rays cascading over the green grass, but it did little to lift her spirits. It was just proof that life went on while her world fell apart. "That's not going to happen. How's Dad?"

"He's coming out of the hospital tomorrow."

Hannah felt some of her tension ease. Her parents' financial woes had so stressed her father that he'd been rushed to the hospital two days earlier due to trouble breathing. Her mother and sister had been certain he was suffering a heart attack because of his weak heart, caused by a construction accident over eleven years ago that left him unable to work. A shady contractor had cut corners on materials used at a site where her father had been working. He ended up falling through two floors of the structure and seriously injuring his back and left hip, leaving him in constant pain. Since then, hospital visits had become part of their lives, as had countless physical therapy sessions.

Fortunately, this time it was just a panic attack, although his blood pressure was dangerously low and he was dehydrated.

Hannah glanced at a tree whose leaves swayed in the slight breeze. "I'll come visit after he's rested a day or two."

"There's no need trying to hide from the inevitable. You can't face them, can you?"

"Of course I can," Hannah said, fighting to take hold of her temper. Her sister was good at igniting it. "I saw them just yesterday. They were fine."

"They were just pretending to make you feel better like they always do," Abigail said, as though her sister was dense. "They don't want to worry the baby of the family."

There was only a five-year age difference between the two sisters, but most of the time it felt like much more. Abigail had wanted to stay an only child and had never welcomed Hannah's arrival. For twenty-eight years she had convinced herself that Hannah was their parents' favorite although they worked hard to treat their daughters as equals—same birthday gifts, same holiday gifts, but nothing seemed to change Abigail's opinion.

Hannah rolled her eyes. "I'll talk to the bank."

"They're going to take the house."

Hannah knew it wasn't that simple. Their home insurance policy had been canceled because the house needed major repairs. She remembered the contractor they'd hired to inspect the house and his quote of over forty-five thousand dollars. If they did not have the repairs done they'd lose their house, and with her father's medical needs that would mean a rehabilitation center or senior residential facility for him—and nobody wanted that.

"I won't let that happen," she said.

"Did you suddenly get rich?"

"No, but—"

"Then how will you stop them?" Abigail's voice cracked. "This is all your fault anyway."

Hannah paused, not sure she'd heard right. "M-my fault?"

"Yes," Abigail said with feeling. "Dad refinanced the house to help you with your education so that you could get your fancy college degree. But instead of graduating and getting a job right away you decided to start your own company. If you had joined an established law firm or something you'd have the money to help. While you were having fun at college I was working to support the family, and now that you're out you *still* can't do anything."

Hannah gritted her teeth. Her sister knew how much earning her degree meant, but every chance she got she belittled her efforts. Abigail knew that Hannah had applied for several jobs and, despite her stellar grades and work experience, hadn't gotten hired. These factors had been part of the decision to start her own law practice. "That's not true, and you know it."

"Why didn't you just join Uncle's business like we all wanted you to? You've worked there since you were sixteen and ran the office like no one else."

"I didn't want to be a secretary."

"There's nothing wrong with being an office assistant."

Hannah kicked a pebble, imagining it was her sister's shin. "I didn't say there was."

"You could have gotten married to Jacob. He has money."

"I'm not ready to get married, especially not to him."

"You're just selfish and—"

"Okay, that's enough. It's not my fault that you're miserable."

"What?"

"You keep blaming me, but in reality you're miserable because you've never left home. You stayed there and watched the house slowly fall down around you and *you* did nothing. After Dad's accident you had an opportunity to travel and didn't. Even though you'd saved your money for a two-week trip to France. Something you'd been talking about since you were nine and saw the movie *An American in Paris.* Dad was doing well then and you could have gone. We all told you to, but you made a choice to stay."

"I couldn't have gone then."

"What about years later?" Hannah continued before her sister could argue. "You chose to stay home and help Mom with Dad. I chose to become a lawyer so that

I could help both my parents and others. So if you're unhappy, that's not my fault. Okay, so I didn't expect things to work out this way. I thought after graduation I'd get a great job and soar high and fast. That didn't happen, because in the real world lots of graduating lawyers don't get work right away. That's the dirty little secret they don't tell you before you enter the profession and get thousands of dollars in debt. I know a guy who graduated top of his class who's waiting tables, and another who's working at his father's car lot. I'm doing the best I can. My business is slowly growing and I'll show you what I can really do, but for now get off my back and find someone else to blame for your unhappiness."

Silence followed and then she heard sniffling. "I didn't mean to make you mad," Abigail said in a tear-soaked voice. "It's just been so hard. Mom and I have done our best to maintain the house, but you know Dad was always the handy one. I've never been good with repairs and things like that. I'm doing all I can, and I'm so scared."

Hannah gripped her phone. With her sister, if it wasn't insults it was tears. "Yes, I know," she said, trying to soften her tone and keep the irritation out of her voice.

"I've spent my life supporting our parents, and I'm helping to take care of Dad. I've done more for them than you ever have…."

Hannah sighed, knowing that she'd never convince her sister to see her in a different light. She knew her sister was as dependent on her parents as they were on her. She'd never ventured out alone, had few friends and had never had any romantic interests. Only in her early thirties, Abigail was resigned to living at home and being provided for. Most times Hannah felt like the older sister because Abigail was never one to offer advice or encouragement.

"It's going to all work out."

"Mom is so worried. We can't imagine having to put Dad into some kind of facility, but if we lose our house no other place will be able to address his needs."

"Look," Hannah said, trying to sound strong, although she didn't feel she had any strength left. She rested against a tree. "I said I'll handle it."

"When?" Abigail pressed, as if she expected her sister to provide a miracle at that moment. "How?"

"Soon."

"How soon?"

Hannah closed her eyes and sighed. "I'll get back to you. I need to go."

"Of course you do. You always have something more important to do than worry about us."

Hannah disconnected and put her phone away, wishing she could do the same with her parents' troubles and her sister's false accusations. She knew what Abigail said wasn't true, but her words hurt anyway. Hannah wanted to be the one to rescue them, and she couldn't. She wanted them to be proud of her, but after graduating from law school she'd ended up with a mountain of debt and no job prospects, and starting her own company was her last-ditch effort. She was getting some clients but not enough to meet all of her financial obligations. Her father's brave smile burned in her memory.

She knew her parents tried to protect her from all their worries, but she'd seen the strain in her mother's eyes and her father had lost a lot of weight. She felt like such a disappointment. When her father had gotten injured on the job, everything changed overnight. She'd been comfortable with the life her family had planned for her. She would work in her uncle's prosperous business, get her degree in business management and perhaps own it one day. But that all changed. She'd returned home from school one day and seen her mother drop the phone and crumble to the floor. She had rushed over to her.

"Is it father?"

"Yes."

"Is he okay?" she asked hesitantly.

"No, he's badly injured."

After her father was hospitalized for over six weeks and had undergone months of physical therapy, they learned that the company he worked for refused to pay for his loss of wages and inability to hold a job. While the lawyer they hired had helped get some compensation for her father, he hadn't been aggressive enough, and her father ended up having to apply for permanent disability, three lawyers later. That's when Hannah decided her new path. She gave up her dream of getting an MBA and running an office. Instead, she'd get justice. She remembered the shock on everyone's face when she told them her plans, but no one would stop her.

She saw what a lawyer could do and knew then that that was what she wanted to strive for. She wanted to use the law to help people get justice. But now she had a law degree, and she couldn't help the ones she cared about the most. Her parents had left Nigeria and worked hard so that she and Abigail could have all the opportunities they couldn't. They had sacrificed for the American Dream, only to be faced with having it all slip away.

Her cell phone rang again and pulled her from her

thoughts. She glanced at the number and groaned. It was Jacob. She couldn't deal with him now. She still felt guilty about their last meeting, when she'd halted several feet from her apartment door trying to figure out how best to handle the man who stood before her holding a bouquet of flowers.

Hannah thought of running but he'd already seen her, so she inwardly groaned and then plastered on a smile and walked toward him. "Jacob, you shouldn't have," she recalled saying to him.

He extended his arm and handed her the flowers. They were beautiful, but the sight of them depressed her. She'd told him that their relationship was over, but he still carried hope and no rebuffs, no matter how hard she tried, could convince him otherwise. He still remembered her and sent her expensive cards on holidays and her birthday. "I told you to stop this."

"I knew you'd be upset about your dad's health scare so I wanted to cheer you up."

It was a likely story, but Hannah didn't completely believe him. "That doesn't matter."

"Okay, I promise. No more flowers."

"Or cards, or teddy bears, or baskets or…"

"Okay," he said, flashing a crooked grin. His smile was both shy and friendly at the same time, and it was one of the reasons she'd fallen for him in the first place. She'd been attracted to his vulnerability. "I get the hint."

Hannah wiped her forehead in an exaggerated gesture of relief. "At last."

"How's your dad?"

"He'll be out of the hospital tomorrow."

"I'm glad to hear that. I care about them like they're my own parents."

Hannah hesitated and then opened her door and turned to him. "They know that, and I'm sure they'd love to see you."

"I needed to see you first."

Hannah rested against the door frame and shook her head. "Jacob, don't do this."

"You know how I feel."

"I really wish you didn't."

"I can't help it."

"You haven't given yourself a chance to. There are many women out there, all much better than me, who deserve a great guy like you."

Jacob hung his head a moment and then smiled at her. "Perhaps if you say that enough times I'll start to believe you."

"Good, because I won't stop."

"So I still don't have a chance?"

"I'm going now."

"You didn't answer my question."

"Because you already know my answer, and it's not going to change. Thanks for the flowers."

"I'd give you a whole lot more if you'd let me."

"Goodbye, Jacob," Hannah said and then closed the door. She set the bouquet on the side table in the foyer and then collapsed on her couch. It had been a hectic day, and she didn't want to end it thinking about how her life may have been different if she'd married Jacob as everyone had expected her to.

She would have lived a life of privilege. Jacob Omole's family was very politically connected in Nigeria and enjoyed state dinners and mingling with the upper crust of society both in Nigeria and among the diplomatic core in Raleigh and D.C., where his parents frequently visited. She'd started dating him in high school. Their families were close. Marriage seemed inevitable to everyone but her. When she'd completed her undergraduate degree she had opted to study abroad in Tanzania, where she worked in a microloan office helping provide needed counseling to women hoping to start a business. Upon returning to the United States she worked as a paralegal for a legal aid program in a poor town in Georgia, where she saw the law work to impact lives. She had had an opportunity to see a bigger world and had larger dreams for her life than the one others had prescribed for her. She chose to follow her heart. Now she just wished she didn't feel so guilty because of it.

Hannah put her phone away, also dismissing the memories of Jacob. She then stumbled over to a park bench and sank into it, feeling as if she was being crushed by the weight of the world. Pain, raw and primitive in its intensity, spread through her, overwhelming her until her throat felt dry and her eyes were blinded by tears. She covered her face and sobbed.

"Hey! I didn't expect to see you here," an exuberant deep voice said from above her.

Her head snapped up and she saw a large, blurry dark figure. She quickly wiped her tears away so she could see him better. The light behind him put him in shadow. She squinted up at him. "I'm sorry?"

"It's good to see you again." He took a seat beside her.

As she brought his face into focus, she realized it was very good to see him, as well. She found herself staring into the caring brown eyes of a handsome man: the man of her dreams.

Chapter 2

He smiled. "How have you been?"

Hannah frowned, wondering why this stranger was smiling so warmly at her. "I'm afraid you've got me confused with someone else," she said, hating to admit it but needing to be honest.

He shook his head. "Impossible. I never forget a pretty face."

Hannah's frown deepened. She was certain she didn't look pretty now with her eyes and nose red from crying. Was he crazy? He didn't look it. He wore a casual pair of khakis, a dark red polo shirt and a gray wool coat draped over one shoulder.

Hannah held up her hand. "How many fingers do you see?"

"Five."

"Strange. I thought you were blind."

Instead of being offended, the man only smiled more

broadly. "A rose with a little dew on its petals doesn't make it any less beautiful."

"You're a poet?"

The man studied her for a moment. "Are you sure you don't remember me?" he asked, sounding disappointed.

"Yes," she said. "I doubt you're the kind of man anyone would forget." She wasn't flattering him. It was a certifiable fact. He was definitely the type of man people noticed. The type who walked into a room and commanded attention. Not because he was the tallest, although he was tall with broad shoulders that exhibited a sleek, taut strength; or the most handsome, although he was that, too. He had a square jaw, dazzlingly brown eyes, warm mocha-brown skin and a bright smile. He had charisma. The kind that exuded from politicians, con men, magicians and playboys. But strangely he didn't seem to be any of those. His interest appeared sincere and genuine, and Hannah found herself falling under his spell even though she didn't want to.

He snapped his fingers. "I know what would jog your memory." He glanced up and saw an ice cream cart. He nodded toward it. "Let me treat you to something sweet." He stood and took her hand, giving her no chance to protest. "Come on."

"But—" Hannah began in a weak voice, shocked not just by his action but also by how comfortable her hand felt in his.

He stopped in front of the vendor and took out his wallet. "Order whatever you want."

She wouldn't say no to free ice cream, even if the man had confused her for someone else. Hannah ordered an ice cream sandwich and he ordered a cone.

His cell phone rang. He glanced at the number.

"You should get that."

"No, it's okay," he said, handing her the sandwich.

"I don't want to keep you."

"You're not. Isn't it a great day?" he said, leaving the vendor a generous tip and walking in the opposite direction.

Hannah fell in line with him. "For some."

"Who's pissing on your parade?"

She laughed. "My sister."

"Older, right?"

Hannah blinked, surprised. "Yes."

He frowned. "That's hard. Any way to get around her?"

"She blames me for everything. My parents might lose their house, and the stress of it put my father in the hospital." Tears welled in her eyes. She sniffed and quickly blinked them away. "I don't know why I'm telling you this, since I don't know you." However, even as she said the words they no longer seemed true. She felt as if she'd known him her whole life. There was an affinity. She trusted him and it felt good to talk to him, to be with him. Suddenly, she was happy that the sun was shining and she could hear the laughter of children in the distance. She noticed the bright white of the spatter of clouds as they slowly drifted across a blue sky that showed no threat of rain.

His phone rang again and he absently turned off its ringer and put it on vibrate.

"What's your name?" she asked, eager to learn more about him.

"Take a guess."

Hannah stroked her chin as if in deep thought. "I know."

"What?"

"Rumpelstiltskin."

He laughed. "That's right. People rarely guess that on the first try."

"Right now I could really use a man who could spin straw into gold," she said, feeling her good mood fading.

The man playfully nudged her with his elbow. "I'm a man of many talents. What do you need?"

"Not me. My parents." Soon she was telling him all about her parents' housing trouble.

"Did you get a second opinion?"

"No."

He wrote down a number. "Call this guy. He's trustworthy. He might be able to give you a lower estimate."

"Thanks. Whom should I say referred him?"

He winked. "Rumpelstiltskin. Call me Rum for short."

Hannah shook her head. "You're impossible." She paused. "Wait. What do you think my name is?"

He hesitated and then suddenly looked sheepish. "I don't remember your name, just your face."

Hannah laughed. "Perhaps I have a twin somewhere." She glanced down at his hand. "Your ice cream is melting."

He looked down and saw the vanilla ice cream leaking from the bottom of his cone onto his hand. He sucked the bottom of the cone until all the ice cream was finished. "There, that's better."

"There's still ice cream on your hand."

"I don't have any napkins."

"Just lick it off."

"Sure." He raised a sly brow. "Want to help me?"

Definitely. She felt her face grow warm. She could imagine licking, sucking, teasing and anything else he asked of her. She bet he tasted sweet, too. She remembered watching the sight of his pink tongue against the chocolate-covered vanilla cone, and just for one wild moment she imagined that chocolate was her skin melting under the warm assault of his tongue. She brushed the thought aside, the day suddenly feeling hotter than it really was. "I still don't know your real name."

"You'll remember it soon."

"Even though you don't remember mine?" she countered.

"At least I remember your face. Your name will come back to me eventually. Of course, you could give me a hint."

Hannah shook her head. "You first. Where did we meet?"

His phone buzzed insistently, as if the caller demanded a response.

"Saved by the bell," she teased, and then she saw an expression of frustration and guilt cross his face. "You really should answer that," Hannah said, seeing his jaw twitch in annoyance. "I'm fine now…really. Thanks for everything."

He glanced at the number and then put the phone away. "I didn't do anything." He lifted her chin with his forefinger. "Keep your chin up." He smiled and then started to walk away.

"Wait. At least tell me your name. What is it?"

He bent down and plucked a buttercup and handed it to her. "You already know it. Just say my name four times and I'll come."

"That's not how the story goes."

"That's how our story will." His mouth spread into a smile that was as intimate as a kiss, and then he turned and walked away.

Hannah watched him go, holding the flower close to her chest, wishing she could hold on to him instead.

"And you didn't get his name?" Hannah's assistant, Bonnie Li, said in disbelief. They sat in Hannah's new office, which was still not completely furnished but serviceable. At least the front receptionist's area looked impressive. She'd had a stroke of luck because one of the tenants in the building where their office was located had just been evicted. They had left behind several pieces of furniture and lamps, which she and Bonnie had eagerly snatched.

The two women had met in college and become fast friends. Like Hannah, Bonnie hadn't lived up to her parents' expectations, either. Small and lithe, she'd trained to be a dancer until a torn ligament ended that dream. Bonnie had a mind to go into sports medicine, which was a profession frowned upon in her Chinese family of three doctors and two university professors. But she'd jumped on board with Hannah despite the low pay, discovering a love for organization and helping people. She looked young for her age of thirty, but she dressed up to appear older. After reading several books on how to make over oneself, she had cut her waist-length black hair short and colored it a striking reddish-brown. She had lovely almond-shaped brown eyes and an attractive slender figure. But there was nothing delicate about her—she liked dirty jokes and the occasional Jack Daniel's. Bonnie pointed at her friend. "What is wrong with you?"

Hannah threw up her hands, helpless. "At first I thought he was crazy. I mean, I looked a mess and he was going on as if he was so happy to see me."

"Tell me how good-looking he was again."

"I've already told you twice."

"Tell me again."

"No, there's no point. I'll probably never see him again."

"Maybe he'll call you."

"He couldn't remember my name, either."

"Maybe he was teasing you."

"Perhaps," Hannah said, doubtful. "But he definitely made my day brighter, especially after my call from Abigail."

Bonnie feigned a shiver of fear. "So, how is the queen of horror?"

Hannah laughed at her friend's description. "She's not that bad."

"No, she's worse. In a horror film she'd be the monster."

"Well, right now she's preparing to be homeless."

"And it's all your fault," Bonnie said, mimicking Abigail's tone.

Hannah nodded, her spirit dimming. "Yes."

"Does she have a reason to really worry this time?"

Hannah sighed. "Unfortunately, yes. It's really looking bad, but I have another option I'm going to try. The guy I met in the park gave me the phone number for another contractor to try. Maybe he can give us a lower estimate."

"It's a start. I hope you get to see him again," Bonnie said, returning to what she was doing.

"Me, too," Hannah said in a soft tone.

* * *

"Where have you been?" Hector Ramirez demanded when Amal stepped into his office. "I've been trying to reach you."

Amal walked past him. "I was busy."

Hector followed him and then paused and studied him with a knowing look. "You met a woman, didn't you?"

Amal shook his head and sat. "It wasn't like that." Hector was a man of thirty-seven with dark eyes and prematurely gray hair that gave him a distinguished look despite his boyish features. Amal liked him, trusted him and rarely kept anything from him. But this time was different.

"I knew it would be a woman."

Amal didn't care what he thought. He wasn't in the mood to discuss it with him. Hector was his trusted friend, but somehow the meeting in the park was something Amal wanted to keep to himself. There was something special about it. He just wasn't sure what yet.

"What line did you use with her?" Hector asked with a smug grin. "How pretty is she? Wait, don't answer—with you they're always gorgeous. Was she a model? An actress? A nurse?"

"No."

"Did you just get her name and phone number, or did you get her address, too?"

"What did you want to tell me?"

Hector paused, flabbergasted that his questions had been ignored. That wasn't typical of Amal. "What? You're not going to tell me about your latest conquest?"

Amal sat back in his chair, keeping his expression

neutral. "I told you it wasn't like that." He held up his hand before Hector could speak. "What's the news?"

Hector sighed. "You're serious? You're not going to tell me anything about this woman?"

Amal slowly blinked and waited.

Hector loosened his tie. Amal was a fun and easygoing guy when he wanted to be, but he could also be a hard SOB when the mood struck him—such as at this moment. He sat and bounced his leg up and down, trying to control his pent-up anxiety and gather the courage to tell him what he knew Amal didn't want to hear. "It's bad."

Amal blinked again, his gaze narrowing slightly.

Hector cleared his throat. His tie was loose, but it still felt as though it threatened to strangle him. "The thing is I—"

"Just tell it to me straight," Amal said, his tone too quiet to be natural.

"The Brenton Law Firm said no."

"I see."

Hector stared at him for a long moment. "That's it? 'I see'? What's wrong with you? It's not like you to be this calm. Are you still thinking about that woman? At least tell me her name in case she calls."

"She's not going to call. Who else is there we can hire?"

"No one."

Amal began to tap a beat on his desk, holding on to his temper. "What do you mean 'no one'?" He wasn't going to let them win. He couldn't. The Walkers wanted to take away everything he'd built with Jade Walker, his former girlfriend. Their business, The Eye of Jade, an art import/export business, had been a success, but unfortunately their relationship had not. He hadn't realized how unstable she was in the beginning. He'd taken her mood swings as part of her vibrant personality and quick mind, although soon her addiction to painkillers following a series of surgeries for a back injury she'd suffered while skiing got out of control. He'd stood by her as she tried rehab after rehab, but nothing helped.

Finally, he had to break free, but it had been hard to leave her. Amal remembered the day they met. He had attended a local fund-raiser for the Raleigh Philharmonic Orchestra's mentoring program that provided musical scholarships to underserved youth in North Carolina. As part of his philanthropic work, Amal donated to several causes and was used to attending these types of functions. On this particular afternoon, he was struck by the striking woman who caught his eye. Now she was dead from an overdose, sixteen months after their breakup. He'd read about it in the papers. It was ruled a suicide, and the Walkers blamed him and wanted him to pay for their loss. But he wasn't going to let them steal away their business. They claimed that the collection of art found in Jade's private storage unit was hers and did not belong to the business. Unfortunately, the last shipment of art she had purchased abroad had been sent to her private storage instead of the company's warehouse, where they usually stored items. This arrangement had been an exception to their normal protocol because Jade had wanted to have pictures taken of the items prior to having them shipped off to the gallery where they were to be displayed.

Unfortunately for Amal, nothing had been put in writing to explain this arrangement, and the Walkers had taken legal action banning him from taking what he believed was his. The gallery owner in New Mexico, where the show was to be held, and the artist, an up-and-coming sculptor, were both threatening to sue. He needed to go to court to refute the Walkers' claim if he didn't want to lose everything.

Hector shifted, uneasy with Amal's silence. "We've gone through twenty law firms and no one will take your case."

Amal started tapping two fingers. "Someone will. Keep digging."

"You want someone ethical, right?"

Amal tapped faster. "I want someone who will win."

Hector swallowed. "All the lawyers in this city know it's career suicide to go up against the Walkers."

"Did you tell them how much I'd pay?"

"They're not interested."

Amal flattened his palm on the desk, his voice low. "Find someone who is."

Chapter 3

At home, Hannah turned on the TV and then glanced at the bouquet of flowers from Jacob sitting on the dining table. When she pulled out her wallet and a crushed flower floated to the floor, she smiled and picked it up. It was the buttercup that the stranger had given her. Its yellow blossom seemed more beautiful than all the flowers in Jacob's bouquet. It made her feel as if she wasn't alone. She took the flower and gently placed it in a page in her journal that she kept nearby. She'd always remember him.

That night Hannah dreamed. She didn't dream about winning the lottery and saving her parents' house or finally convincing Jacob that he was better off without her, or finding a way to get along with her sister. No, she dreamed about him. The Stranger. She'd tried to come up with a name for him, but nothing seemed to suit him. Paul seemed too pedantic. Armando too exotic. So to her he was just The Stranger. The Handsome Stranger, that aspect of him she couldn't refute—those captivating brown eyes and beautifully etched features.

She imagined walking and talking with him in the park again.

Hannah dreamed about him the next night, too, and the one after that, each time her dreams becoming more detailed and more intimate. Dreams were safe, and she couldn't get hurt. Soon she no longer met him in the park, but for dinner and then she was in his arms. There she always felt safe. Cared for. It was nice to have someone to lean on. And he always said the right thing, encouraging her as he had in the past. Lifting her up. Making her feel like a success when only seconds before she'd felt like a failure. She remembered the feel of her hand in his, the touch of his hand on her skin. She imagined it on her arm, caressing her face, sliding down her body.

She hadn't noticed a ring, but a guy like that wouldn't be single. Even if he was…with her luck she'd likely never meet him again. A week later she went back to the park on the same day they'd met, hoping it was a habit of his to be there. She waited two hours on the same park bench with no luck. She felt foolish knowing that part of her wanted to see him so that her dreams could stop and she could face the reality of him. Still, a part of her liked him just being her dream man. Relationships weren't her specialty anyway, and not seeing him again was probably for the best.

Across town Amal was also thinking about her, but not in the same way or for the same reason. She came into his mind quite unexpectedly as he tried to gently break up with his present girlfriend, Evie, who'd convinced herself that they were destined to be married. There had been signs early in their relationship. After the first date, she'd already started talking about marriage, babies and how "Mrs. Evie Harper" would look great on personalized stationery and matching towels.

They hadn't been dating long. Unfortunately, Amal hadn't realized that it was a rebound relationship to help him forget about Jade. He did not love Evie and did not want to lead her on much longer.

"What do you mean I'm too good for you?" she demanded, tears streaming down her face, her nose red. Clearly, her makeup wasn't waterproof, because two black streaks stained her cheeks. She was still a beautiful woman with hazel eyes and curly short hair who was a magician at event planning and worked for a company that organized national conventions held in Raleigh.

Amal quickly glanced around, aware of heads turning, sending him curious and judging glances. He'd thought that by taking her to a restaurant it would stop her from creating a scene. He'd guessed wrong. "Just that," he said, keeping his voice soft and measured, "I'm not ready to settle down. I told you that."

Evie dabbed at her eyes, smudging her makeup more and making her look as if she had a black eye. "I thought I could change your mind."

"I'm no good for you."

"You're perfect for me. I knew I'd lose a guy like you. You can get any woman you want. Is there someone else?"

"No."

"Then just give me another chance."

"It's not going to work." Amal tried to get the waitress's attention, but she was busy checking out her lipstick in the reflection of a spoon.

"I love you, Amal."

"You hardly know me."

"I know you enough."

Amal glanced up again, wanting to throw a bread roll or something at the absentminded waitress so that he could pay the check and leave. He stopped another passing waiter. "I want to pay my bill."

The waiter glanced at Evie, concerned. "Is everything all right?"

"My life is over," Evie whined.

Amal gritted his teeth. "The food was so delicious, it made her cry. Now, I'd like my bill, please."

"Yes, sir."

"You're angry with me," Evie said.

Amal drummed his fingers on his thigh. "No, I'm not."

"I can always tell when you're angry. Your eyes narrow and your jaw twitches."

Amal counted to ten.

"I hate when you're angry with me," she said and then burst into tears.

Amal silently swore, wishing he'd gotten a private booth instead of just a table. He moved his chair closer and pulled her near his side to hold her. He didn't care what those around him were thinking. Let everyone stare. Most already were. "It's okay." He hated to see a woman cry. And that's when his mind floated to the woman who'd been crying alone, sitting on the park bench. For some reason her tears and misery bothered him more than Evie's. Maybe because with Evie, he was relieved at finally letting her know there was no chance of them being together, or the fact that he knew she'd get over him quickly.

The woman in the park smelled sweet and there was a heaviness he understood. She didn't seem like the type to normally cry in public, although he could be wrong. But he'd felt helpless and had come up with the story that he knew her just to make her feel better. He was happy he'd been able to make her smile. He wondered how she was doing and if she'd been able to save her parents' house.

"Amal?"

He blinked and glanced down. He'd totally forgotten about Evie even though she was wetting his shirt with tears. "Huh?"

"Did you even hear a word I said? Don't you care about me at all?"

"Of course I do. But this is for the best." He glanced at his watch. It was time to go. Besides, he was hoping to drop her off before the evening news started. And he'd make sure to never come to this restaurant again.

"How did it go?" his mother, Doreen Harper, asked the moment he walked through the door. She sat on the couch holding a glass. A plate of cookies sat on the coffee table. She noticed his pointed look and smiled. "Relax. It's just water, dear."

"Mixed with what?"

"Nothing."

"Hmm."

"And I'm not using it to wash anything down, either."

Amal was relieved but didn't say so. His mother lived with him because he didn't trust her on her own. She'd overcome an addiction to prescription pills, but was still susceptible to drinking more than she could handle and men attracted only to her money. She even looked like an easy target, with wide brown eyes, a petite build, easy smile and expensive clothing and jewelry. "I don't wear paste," she claimed when he'd once scolded her for wearing a ten-thousand-dollar necklace on a Manhattan subway. She'd been pampered and sheltered all her life until her husband decided to leave her with a small son. She always had money, but never had to manage it on her own.

At age ten, Amal became in charge of the household finances, stopping anyone, from the gardener to the chef, from robbing his mother blind. She'd gotten into prescription pills to deal with the stress of her divorce. Thankfully, she'd conquered it by the time he was in college. But four years ago when a pool maintenance guy had convinced her to marry him, which did not happen thanks to Amal's swift intervention, she had gone back to drinking. Amal had to step in again to keep an eye on her. Luckily, his then-girlfriend, Jade, hadn't minded. He knew he couldn't have her close by forever, but Amal had the space and didn't mind the company, especially when everything else seemed to be going against him.

Doreen took a sip of her water and then set it down. "You haven't answered my question."

"How do you think it went?"

"From the look on your face, not well."

Amal sat on the couch in front of her and then took a cookie from her plate. "She thought we were going to get married."

"And of course you're never going to get married."

"I've never said that."

"You don't have to. If she'd had half a brain, she would have seen it written all over your face. Didn't I tell you that you should have married Jade when you had the chance? Then you wouldn't be in this mess. Marriage makes things legal."

Amal rested his head back and gazed up at the ceiling. "Thirty-two."

"What?"

He sat up and stared at her. "That's the number of times you've said 'I told you so' over the past year."

Doreen set her glass down with regret. "I'm sorry. I just hate seeing you keep making these mistakes. I told you Evie was no good."

"Yes."

"And that she was desperate."

Amal drummed his fingers on his thigh. "I know."

"And that pathetic woman before her. I said she was only after your money."

He sighed and drummed faster. "I know."

"Since Jade, your taste in women has taken a dive."

Amal stopped drumming and shook his head. "No, not my taste. Just my luck. Don't worry. I'm not interested in another relationship. I'm through with women for now."

Doreen started to laugh.

"You think that's funny?"

"I think that's impossible. The moment you started nursing I knew you were straight."

Amal squeezed his eyes shut, embarrassed. "Mom!"

"It's true. You've always loved women and everything about them."

"From now on I promise I'll enjoy them from afar." He pointed at her. "Stop laughing. I'm serious."

"You're trying to be, but it's not working."

"I mean it. My only focus is winning this case against the Walkers. Until it's through I'm off the market."

"Unless she has the right dimensions," Doreen said, cupping the air.

"Don't be crass. You're my mother."

"Grow up. I'm also a woman who knows how men think," Doreen said with a smirk. "Especially you, my dear boy. I know all your weak spots."

Yes, he had weak spots, and one of them had been Jade. He'd made mistakes, but he wouldn't let the Walkers exploit them. What his mother hadn't realized was how much winning meant to him, and no woman would stand in his way. "I'm not going to let the Walkers take away everything Jade and I built together. She wouldn't want that."

"So you've finally found a lawyer?"

"I will."

Doreen picked her up her glass and finished its contents as if it were a lot stronger than water. "I've asked around and no one is interested. I'm not sure you can win this with your inventory tied up. The Walkers are going to play hardball. It's going to cost you a lot of money. I can take care of you until you get back on your feet."

"No way. I'm not having you bail me out of this. I'm going to win. I'm offering a lot of money. I'll find someone who will bite."

Hannah looked at the prices on the menu and winced. The only things within her budget were the water and breadsticks. She knew the price didn't cover just the cost of the food, but also the ambience and the waterfront view. She glanced up at her two friends, glad that they were focused on their orders so she had more time to decide what to do. Dana Wentworth had a name that hinted at white Anglo-Saxon Protestant breeding and generations of wealth, but she was born in Queens to a Jewish deli owner and his Catholic Italian wife. She had olive-toned skin, dark green eyes and a full figure that she always dressed well. She'd worked her way from New York City into the suburbs of North Carolina, although none of her family could understand her interest in living in the South. She'd made a nice life as a corporate lawyer in a prestigious firm. Natasha Petrov was a Russian immigrant whose poor parents had sent her to live with wealthy relatives in Missouri, who had adopted her as their own. Blonde and slender, she'd married a wealthy man, so price was never an issue. Although she didn't need the money, she worked part-time in family law. They'd remained friends after law school, although their lives had taken divergent paths. Hannah wondered if she'd be able to meet with them anymore.

"The salmon salad looks delicious," Dana said.

Natasha shook her head. "No, I think I'll have the chicken primavera."

"What about you, Hannah?"

"Oh, I'll just have tea and um…"

"The risotto."

"No, I—"

"You'll love it," Natasha said. "Trust me. I had it here before," she said with a quick flick of her wrist, the light catching her large diamond wedding ring.

Hannah only smiled, imagining twenty bucks she was going to use to pay an overdue bill bursting into flames.

The food arrived and the three friends discussed different topics, including Natasha's recent visit to Russia, Dana's work woes and Hannah's family troubles, although she didn't reveal too much.

"Oh," Dana said. "You won't believe what news has been circulating in the legal gossip chain. Some crazy playboy is in an estate battle with the Wild Walkers."

"An estate battle?" Hannah asked.

"Yes, but here's the kicker. He doesn't have a lawyer and he's been going around town offering a boatload of money for anyone to take his case."

"And no one will?" Hannah asked with interest. The new contractor the stranger from the park had referred had given her a lower estimate for fixing her parents' house. Unfortunately, it was still too much for their budget, even with what little she could help them with.

"Not if you want to have a career in law. The Walkers are brutal."

"Yes," Natasha said. "Remember the case The Walkers versus Baldano Flooring Company? They put them out of business."

"What's the guy's name?" Hannah asked.

Natasha grabbed her friend's arm. "You're not thinking of—"

Dana shook her head. "Hannah, I know you want a juicy case, but this isn't the one to start with."

"Just tell me his name," Hannah said.

Dana looked at Natasha, who shrugged. "She'd find out anyway," she said.

"It's Amal Harper."

"Amal Harper. That name sounds vaguely familiar."

"It should be more than familiar. He's the owner of The Eye of Jade, the classy art company that has extravagant art shows and sells unique art pieces from around the world."

"So he has a lot of money."

"For now. Once the Walkers are finished with him, he may have to move out of state just to get a job working in a fast-food chain."

"Don't do it," Natasha said.

"I didn't say I would," Hannah replied. "I'm just curious."

"Said the cat on the last day of her nine lives," Dana said in a grim tone.

Usually Hector didn't like surprises, but that Thursday afternoon was an exception. He stared at the phone, picking it up and putting it down twice just to make sure it was real and that he wasn't dreaming. He felt like dancing around the room. But he knew he couldn't get too happy because he had to find out more about Hannah Olaniyi before he told Amal. She was interested in handling his case. What if she wasn't up to the task? Or what if she was just in it for the money? Then it would be a wasted effort. But at least this was a start.

"Who is it?"

He spun around and stared at Amal, who'd come into the office carrying a large brown folder. "What?" he said, feigning innocence.

A grin tugged on Amal's mouth. "Don't try to hide it. You're happy about something." He pointed the folder at him as a thought came to mind. "You found someone."

"I may have," Hector said, determined to temper his joy with caution.

Amal sat on the edge of the desk. "You did. Who?"

"I got a call from the assistant to Hannah Olaniyi.

She's interested in helping you with the estate battle. I was going to tell you, but I thought I should find out more about her first. She wasn't on my list, and few people know about her."

"Which means she is new and hungry."

"Or new and naive," Hector corrected, not wanting Amal to get ahead of himself. "Or better yet, doesn't have the skill we need to win. First let me—"

"Did you say yes?"

"I thought we should meet with her first and—"

Amal lifted the receiver and handed it to him. "Call back and accept."

Hector set it back down. "But—"

"There are three things I already like about her. She heard about the case and called us about it. She offered her services without you trying to persuade her."

"And three?"

"She's a woman." He grinned. "I like to work with women."

Hector groaned. "You told your mother you were staying away from women to focus on the case."

"You've been talking to my mother?"

"She wants me to keep an eye on you."

"And?"

"And what?"

He waited.

Hector sighed. "All right. We have a little wager that you'll be involved with a woman within two weeks maximum."

"Nice to know you have such faith in me."

"I said three, but I know you."

Amal held up his hands and wiggled his fingers. "I'll be able to look but not touch."

"Right," Hector said, hoping Ms. Olaniyi wasn't Amal's type, or he'd be out a hundred dollars.

"He said he'd get back to us," Bonnie said as Hannah paced the room.

"Are you sure you sold me enough?"

"Yes."

"Did you tell him I was called the barracuda on my debate team and that—"

"I said all the right things. I think he sounded really excited but tried to hide it. I'm sure he'll call back tomorrow, but he doesn't want to seem too eager."

Hannah chewed her lower lip. "Yes, I'm sure that's it."

The phone rang. They stared at each other and then Bonnie picked up.

"Yes? Okay. Okay. That's fine. Thank you. Goodbye." She hung up.

Hannah stared at her with her heart pounding. "Well?"

Bonnie jumped out of her chair. "You've got the case. They want to meet Monday and discuss the details." The two women screamed and hugged each other and then Hannah sobered.

"Hmm…shouldn't we have scheduled the meeting?"

"He says his boss likes to be in charge."

"Fine. As long as his checks don't bounce he can schedule to his heart's content. This is great. This gives me time to find out more about him and the Walkers."

Finding out about the Walkers wasn't hard. They were from old money and had lived in the area for over one hundred years. Their money had been earned through the banking industry and investment in real estate, including the ownership of several high-rise buildings in the middle of downtown Raleigh. They were the cornerstone of the establishment and were known for their philanthropic activities, including donating to the development of a new wing at the local children's hospital and the new Ronald McDonald house for parents of children being treated with life-threatening illnesses. The annual Walker golf championship, held in the spring, was an event Hannah and all of the citizens in the community were aware of. The event brought together a variety of dignitaries and stars and raised several million dollars for not-for-profit organizations in the area. Hannah exhausted herself poring over the unlimited news articles and pictures she found online.

"He's a real good-looking guy," Bonnie said, staring at the computer screen. "Come and look."

Hannah brushed the comment away with a wave of her hand. "I don't care what he looks like. Just give me the facts."

Bonnie did. He liked the nightlife and the company of beautiful women. Attended charity events, but whether out of philanthropy or to be seen wasn't clear. He'd never married and clearly didn't seem ready to march down the aisle anytime soon.

"I don't care who he is…. He's the answer to my prayers."

Hannah dressed her best that Monday. She wanted to make a good impression even though she knew she had the upper hand since no one else wanted the case. She felt the case itself would be a struggle based on the information she'd read about the Walkers and since it was her first, but she was ready for the challenge. She sat at her desk and waited.

Then she heard voices and a knock on her door. She straightened, and in walked the man from her dreams.

Chapter 4

Amal halted in the doorway when he saw her. He noticed the surprise and amazement on her pretty face and nearly took a step back. He had to play it cool. He didn't want anything to jeopardize her representing him. He had to remain in control even though he didn't feel as if he was. Instead, he felt as if his world had tilted on its axis and that nothing would be the same again. His throat constricted, his mouth felt parched and his heart acted as if it wanted to beat out of his chest. He took a deep breath, glad he still knew how to breathe. He fought not to remember the scent of her perfume or notice how the color of her lime-green suit looked against her skin. He tried to ignore how the light revealed reddish highlights in her hair and how when she licked her lips he wanted to lick them, too. No, he had to focus on the case. That was all that mattered right now.

He held out his hand, pleased by how firm and steady

it looked. Yes, he could do this. "It will be a pleasure to work with you."

"Yes," Hannah said in a rush. "Will you excuse me?" She darted out of the room, pushing past him on her exit, allowing him another whiff of her floral scent. He gripped his hands into fists.

Hector spun around, sending him an accusatory look. "What have you done?"

Amal took a seat, setting his briefcase down. "I haven't done anything."

"She looked at you as if she'd seen a ghost or something. Please don't tell me she's a former conquest you've forgotten about."

"I never forget a woman."

"It can happen."

"Not to me. Besides, she's never been one of mine. And will you stop calling them *conquests?*"

"I say it out of admiration."

"I don't care."

"Fine," Hector reluctantly conceded, "but something's wrong, and I need to find out what. I don't like surprises. They are never good."

Amal tugged on his cuffs and grinned. "My little optimist."

"I'm serious."

"I'm sure it's nothing."

"She's the only one willing to help us. We can't lose her."

The thought made Amal's stomach clench. Now that he'd found her again, he didn't want to lose her, but he wouldn't think about why. "We're not going to," Amal said with a confidence he didn't feel.

* * *

Hannah locked herself in the bathroom stall, wanting to jump up and down and scream. She just kicked the door instead. He was here. The man she'd been dreaming about for many nights was here and was quickly becoming her worst nightmare. He wasn't the caring, generous and wonderful man she'd imagined him to be. Instead, he was a conniving playboy who went through women as he did his shirts. He'd likely used one of his lines to get her attention that day in the park. She wondered how often he used that line. Obviously it was effective; she'd fallen for it—and him—completely. From Bonnie's research she knew he never settled with one woman for too long, especially after breaking up with Jade Walker. She felt like a fool. She banged her head against the door, welcoming the pain in her head. It was better than the one seeping into her heart.

He'd probably laughed about how easy it had been to manipulate her. But she wouldn't think about that. She needed the job. She didn't need to like him. And he didn't need to know how she'd felt about him. What he thought about her didn't matter as long as she got paid. He'd probably forgotten all about it anyway. She'd be professional and distant.

She heard a knock on the door and then Bonnie's worried tone. "Hannah? Are you all right?"

Hannah wiped her eyes and came out. "I'm fine."

"Did he say something? Do you want me to be in on the meeting?"

"No, I can handle Mr. Harper."

Hannah returned to her office and stared at Amal— seeing the steely jaw and cunning gaze. She hadn't seen that before, but she wouldn't forget it now.

"Okay, let's get to work."

They discussed the case and then finished for the day.

"Will you excuse us?" Amal said to Hector as they prepared to leave.

"Are you sure?" Hector said.

Amal sent him a cutting look. Hector hesitated and then left.

Once he'd closed the door, Amal leaned forward and softened his voice. "It's nice to see you again, Hannah."

"Is it?" she said, sounding bored.

"I think so."

"So now you remember my name?"

"It suits you."

"Stop playing games with me."

"I'm not playing games."

"You lied to me. In the park you said we'd met before, but when I just saw you, you were just as surprised to see me as I was to see you. Why is that? You knew my name and what I did, yet you were just as shocked when you saw me. That means you've never heard of or seen me before."

He shrugged. "Okay, so I lied."

Hannah blinked, amazed by how comfortable he was admitting it. "Why? You wanted to get my number or something? Or perhaps you were just bored that day and wanted to see if you could toy with me. I know all about you. I know how you think getting women in bed should be an Olympic sport."

"I've never said that."

"There's no need to. Your actions speak loud enough."

"You shouldn't believe everything you read."

"Or everything you hear." She folded her arms, wanting to look unmoved, although she was feeling so many emotions she could hardly keep still. "Why did you lie?"

"I wanted to make you stop crying."

Hannah paused, hating how he was a constant surprise to her. "I don't believe you."

He shrugged. "It's the truth. Did the contractor give you a good estimate?"

"No."

"Oh. Look, a friend owes me a favor. I can get your parents' house fixed so they'll get insured."

Hannah held up her hand and shook her head. "I don't need your help. You're the one who needs mine."

Amal shrugged and leaned against her desk. "I don't see why you're so upset. It was a harmless diversion." He continued before she could reply, "Did I try to get your number or address?"

"No."

He folded his arms. "You're lucky I didn't have to resort to plan B."

"Plan B?"

"Yes." He came around the desk and lifted her to her feet. "I was going to kiss you." And then he did just that. She expected to be repelled, alarmed, violated, but instead the touch of his lips on hers was like coming home. Like the sweet smell of cinnamon pancakes on a Sunday morning, or the sound of a crackling fire on a still winter's night. He felt safe, secure, right. Although her body wanted to believe that, her mind refused to. He was all wrong for her—too many smooth lines and charming smiles.

Hannah shoved him away and wiped his kiss from her mouth. "If you ever do that again—" She stopped at the sight of the stunned expression on his face—

wonder, amazement, confusion and a slight hint of fear. All that she'd felt. But she brushed the thought aside. They were nothing alike. She snapped her fingers in his face. "Did you hear me?"

He blinked as though waking from a trance. "I'm sorry. I was out of line." He rubbed the back of his neck and sighed. "I don't know what has gotten into me."

"Your ego is the size of a continent."

"Relax." He sat on the corner of her desk. "I'm not hitting on you. You're not even my type."

"Lucky me," she said in a dry tone.

He cringed, looking uneasy, which seemed like an uncharacteristic trait for him. "I didn't mean it like that. All I'm saying was that I was trying to help you and I would have done whatever it took to make you smile."

"Fine," Hannah said in clipped tones. "Let's forget it."

"Do you trust me?"

"What?"

"I need to know whether you trust me or not. I need you to believe in my case and fight for me."

"I will."

"That's not what I asked you."

Hannah sat behind her desk and met his stare. "But that's what I'm telling you."

He sat and glared at her with an intensity that made a tinge of fear slither down her spine. He kept his voice measured and controlled. "The Walkers are good and they are going to paint a portrait of me that's—" he hesitated "—less than savory. If you already believe them, there's no point in you representing me. No, I'm not a saint. But I built my company with Jade and I did love her and I tried to be everything she wanted me to be, but it wasn't enough. I didn't callously abandon her, and I was not the reason she committed suicide. If you think that's the kind of man I am then let's end this partnership now."

"I'll take the case."

"Wrong answer." He stood.

"You need me."

"Not that bad."

Hannah jumped to her feet, seeing the answer to her parents' problem walking out the door. "I can take your case without having to like you."

"No, you can't." Amal grabbed the door handle.

She rushed over to him and stopped him from opening the door. "Okay, wait. I believe you."

Amal gazed down at her with a blank expression, making it hard for her to read him. "About everything?" he challenged in the same measured tone. "And be careful how you answer."

"Yes."

"And you like me?"

"I'll work on it."

"I know you're a lawyer, but you shouldn't lie to me."

"Lie?"

"Yes." He opened the door then winked at her, making her heart skip a beat although she wanted to slap him. "I know you like me. You just have to get used to the idea."

Hannah was too stunned to reply, and by the time she had a cutting retort, he and Hector were gone.

She needed the money. That's all that mattered. Hannah tried to remind herself that saving her parents' house was worth the risk of dealing with a playboy and going against a powerful family that could cost her her career.

"Isn't this great?" Bonnie said, rushing up to her.

Hannah returned to her desk, masking her jumbled feelings. "What's great?"

"This case. It's exciting and you get to work with Amal Harper. If you win, you'll never want for clients again."

Hannah picked up a pen and waved it at her friend in warning. "The word being *if*."

Bonnie frowned. "It's not like you to be negative."

"I know," Hannah said, holding her head for a moment. She let her hands fall to the desk. "I'm just a little overwhelmed. I hope I haven't taken on too much."

"You haven't." Bonnie suddenly looked thoughtful. "You know, he's better-looking than his photos."

"And you mention that because…?"

"I wouldn't blame you."

"Wouldn't blame me for what?"

"If something's going on."

Hannah widened her eyes. "Nothing is. Why would you say that?"

"Just the way you were looking at each other."

"We met briefly before, but trust me, it's nothing."

Bonnie sat and crossed her legs, swinging one foot. "No, it's not."

"He's a client."

Bonnie began to grin. "He won't be a client forever."

"I'm not his type and he's not mine. End of story," Hannah said, sending her friend a long, firm look that didn't allow any contradictions.

"If you say so," Bonnie said, clearly not believing her but wise enough to let the subject drop.

* * *

The moment Hannah got home she went into her bedroom, opened her diary and stared at the carefully preserved buttercup Amal had given her, wondering if she should tear it into pieces.

She slammed her diary shut and shoved it away from her as she sat on her bed. She wanted to rip it up, but she couldn't because even though she knew the truth about the man, she couldn't erase the memory of how he'd made her feel that day. She opened her diary again and gazed at the flower, lightly touching it with her finger. She'd keep it as a reminder as to why she needed to focus on work instead of men. Work she could always depend on and trust. Work didn't let her down or disappoint her. She wouldn't let herself get distracted by a man who'd made it an art of stealing women's hearts. Not that she was in danger of that since she wasn't his type anyway. *You're not my type.* She wished his words made her more angry than upset, but they'd forced her to look at the mirror and face the truth of what he'd said.

From the pictures she'd seen of him at numerous parties and events, she knew he usually went for those classically beautiful African American ladies with long hair and tiny waists. Or Caucasian women with wide eyes and long legs. Delicate beauties who looked as if the slightest breeze would make them crumble. Not medium-height women with short black hair and West African features. She knew she was attractive, but no one would mistake her for an American with her exotic features—dark eyebrows and lashes, cupid-bow lips, a sleek, long neck and dark brown skin.

In school she didn't look like the other kids, but her parents, uncles and aunts always showed her how beautiful she was and surrounded her with images of women like her. In travels she'd turned men's heads while dining in Portugal and sailing in Barbados.

She put on a deep royal-red lipstick and her favorite pair of earrings and again stared at her reflection in the mirror. She was a beautiful woman and plenty of men thought so, and Amal was blind if he didn't see it, whether she was his type or not. She blew herself a kiss. She was a great daughter and a caring friend, and she'd save her parents' home and show Mr. Amal Harper the kind of top-notch lawyer she was.

You're not my type. What the hell was wrong with him? He'd never been so tactless with a woman before. Especially a beautiful one. Amal jogged around the gym track, the conversation he'd had with Hannah repeating in his mind. He wanted to forget his words, but even more he wanted to forget his actions and his response to her. He never would have imagined she would have tasted so good, her mouth as soft as warm butter melting on freshly baked bread. He got hard just thinking about her. That wasn't like him. No, she wasn't his type and she couldn't be. He wouldn't let her, although part of him wanted to take the risk. He'd liked that he'd been able to make her smile, that she'd known nothing about him in the park and had liked his company anyway. He hadn't felt so relaxed and carefree in years. But that didn't matter. Now he needed her solely for business.

"I thought I'd find you here," Hector said, jogging up beside him.

Amal didn't reply. He came to the gym to think, not to talk.

"So...you two don't have anything going on between you, right?"

"Right."

"Good."

"Why do you say *good* like that?"

"I like her."

"Who?"

"Hannah."

"Hmm."

"And I want to ask her out."

Amal halted. "What?"

Hector kept jogging. "I want to ask her out."

Amal caught up to him, his voice firm. "You're not dating my lawyer."

"Why not? She's free. While you were talking to her, I learned from her assistant that she's not seeing anyone."

"She's not free to see you or anybody."

"You can't stop her from dating."

"She'll be busy enough with me. I want her focused on my case and nothing else."

"And no one else," Hector added.

Amal shook his head. "I'm not interested in her that way. This is purely business."

"She's an attractive woman."

Amal remained silent.

"And I saw the way you were looking at her," Hector pressed.

"It's not what you think."

"I don't need your permission on whom I date."

"No, but if you still want to have a place to work you'll reconsider. Take her off the menu."

"I'll give you my two weeks' notice."

"Your resignation is rejected."

"What?"

"You heard me."

"It's not like you to keep secrets from me. This woman is important and I want to know why."

Amal released a fierce sigh. "Hell, even I don't know why, all right? I met her in the park. She was going through a rough time and I bought her some ice cream, that's all. I like my life simple. I'm not going to get involved with her and neither are you, because I don't want the possibility of relationship drama. Do I make myself clear?"

Hector kept jogging but didn't reply.

Chapter 5

Hector knew he was taking a gamble, but he was up for it. He wanted to see Hannah again and find out more about her. He was certain he didn't have a chance, but something about her made her seem approachable. He wanted to know what Amal's interest was, too. He knew there was more going on between them, and he didn't like being kept in the dark. But he had to play it cool and not appear overly eager.

He pushed back his hair and adjusted his tie and then walked into the office, trying to mimic the swagger women found so attractive in Amal. He stopped at the reception desk, where Hannah's assistant sat. He opened his mouth, but she gave him one quick look and then shook her head. "Sorry, but you won't do."

"What?"

"You don't have an appointment, do you?" she asked, sounding as if she already knew the answer.

"No, but—"

"You just dropped by to say hello?"

"Yes," he stammered. "Something like that."

She shook her head, giving him a pitying glance. "I don't blame you for being interested in her, but you're all wrong."

Hector felt himself getting angry. What right did she have to judge him? He was reasonably good-looking with a great job, and he knew how to treat a woman right.

She began to grin. "I hit a nerve, didn't I?"

"Is Hannah in or not?"

"No," Bonnie said. "There are three reasons you're wrong for her. You're too kind. She has a sister who would eat you up for a snack. Secondly, she needs someone to stand up for her even though she doesn't know it, and lastly—" She stopped and softly swore, staring at something behind him. Hector turned and saw a man enter the office.

"Can I speak to Hannah?" the man asked.

"She's not in."

"Do you know when she will be?"

"No."

"I can't reach her on her cell."

Bonnie just shrugged.

"Is it true she's going to take on the Walkers?"

"You'll have to wait and hear that from her."

"Fine. Tell her—"

"That you stopped by," Bonnie finished as if she'd done so many times. "I will, Jacob. Like always."

He left.

"That guy won't get the hint," Bonnie said under her breath.

"Who is he?"

"Your competition."

"I thought she wasn't seeing anybody."

"She isn't, but everyone expects her to eventually marry him. They dated. He's got everything going for him and it would take a lot of gumption to convince her family you're a more suitable choice."

"I just wanted a date, not to marry her."

"Look, Hannah needs a man who will stand by her. She briefly dated one guy other than Jacob but the stress of her life was too much for him and he went running. She doesn't need another heartbreak like that. This is a difficult time in her life. You're not the man for her. But you're in luck."

"Luck?"

"Yes." She winked. "Fortunately, you're just the guy for me."

He blinked.

She rested her chin in her hand and fluttered her eyelashes. "Feel free to ask me out anytime."

He hesitated. It wasn't what he'd expected, but he knew a choice opportunity when he saw one. "There's a café you may like. Would you——"

"I'd love to." She grinned and Hector soon felt himself grinning back.

Amal pounded his pillow with his fist and then used it to cover his face. He couldn't sleep. He never had a problem sleeping. Usually the moment he turned off the lights and his head hit the pillow he was out for the night. But not this time. This time he was wide-awake, and it was all because of *her*. Hannah. He couldn't stop thinking about her. It didn't make any sense. What made

her so special? Okay, so their first meeting had been nice, but he'd met plenty of women and none had affected him the way she did. What was wrong with him?

He couldn't stop remembering kissing her, the feel of her hair against his face. He recalled their first meeting and the way he'd been able to make her face light up with a smile. He'd had the same pride and excitement as a virginal teen on his first date. But she wasn't the first. Not by a long shot. But his brief time with her lingered in his mind like the sweet taste of honeysuckle, a pleasure that was too short. She'd looked at him as just an ordinary man. His money, his wealth, his background didn't matter. She'd liked him without knowing his name or what he did or what he could do for her.

Amal tossed the pillow aside and sighed. That was over. Now his reputation was all she saw and all she cared about. Perhaps it was for the best, because he couldn't be interested in her. He didn't like what he felt. It was too real, too deep, and it could be addictive— that sweetness, that feeling of rightness. But he wasn't right for anyone. Jade had taught him that. He wouldn't get tied down again. He wouldn't try to be what someone else needed him to be. He'd just have fun. He liked being a free man and would remain free no matter what.

Martha Walker looked at her assistant with a steady gaze. She could maintain such a gaze with the calm patience of a cheetah stalking its prey. A woman of sixty-three, she looked a decade younger, with short dyed black hair and light brown eyes. She was a heavy-set woman but moved as though she were fifty pounds lighter, and dressed with excellent care. She sat in her

living room, having finished her afternoon snack. "What did you just say?"

"He found someone," her assistant, Peter Lawford, said with a note of boredom. He did boredom well. He was an attractive man with a muscular build and short brown hair, but Martha still didn't particularly like him. However, he was good at his job and uncomplicated. He didn't have a social life—taking no obvious interest in either men or women—so he was always available to her.

Martha paused. "Are you sure?"

Peter sighed as if he were about to yawn, but just glanced out the window. "My sources don't lie."

"Who?"

He shifted his gaze to her. "Some woman with a foreign name. No one remarkable."

Martha sniffed. Figures Amal would get a woman. No man would be foolish enough to take his case. "Find out everything you can about her."

"I'm already on it. From what we know she hasn't been out of law school for too long."

"A recent graduate? Then she'll be more easily persuaded to quit this silly game."

Peter lifted an eyebrow, expressing curiosity. "If she's under Amal's spell it may be harder than you think."

Martha shook her head. "No, I'm able to break his spell. Just give me the information I want and leave the rest to me."

"Yes, the situation is being taken care of," Hannah said to her sister on her cell phone as she walked to her apartment complex. "I just spoke with the mortgage company and the bank. You're not going to be homeless."

"What are you going to do?"

"Does it matter as long as it works? What could go wrong?" She abruptly stopped when a man stepped in her path. No, more than a man—a vision. He was beautifully made with dark ebony skin, light brown hair and a fit physique. He looked like the kind of man who didn't need to expend much energy to get what he wanted. She took a step back and made a move to the right. He moved with her.

"Hannah Olaniyi?" he said in a bored tone, as if he were asking her the recent price of bread.

She paused, surprised that he knew her full name and that he could say her surname with ease. "Yes?"

"Get in the car."

Hannah looked at the black limo he gestured to. "Abigail, I'll call you back."

"What's going on?" her sister demanded.

"I'll tell you later."

"I knew something bad would happen. I think—"

Hannah disconnected and put her cell phone away. "You forgot to say please."

"Please get in the car."

"And why would I do that?"

"To make our lives easier," the gorgeous man said with a tired sigh. He lowered his voice and opened the door. "Trust me, you don't want to fight me on this. Just get in."

Hannah measured his size. "I was a runner in college," she said.

"I was state champion."

"Karate?"

"Wrestling champ, too," he said, sounding amused.

"Hmm." Hannah knew she wouldn't be able to topple or outrun him, so her options were few. She playfully patted him on the cheek, wanting to shock him and succeeding when his eyes widened a fraction. "Since you asked so nicely." She ducked inside the limo and sat, only to find herself in front of an elegant older woman with a steely gaze of disapproval. Hannah found her lovely features vaguely familiar. She wondered if the woman expected her to curtsy or bow, but she didn't wonder for long since she didn't intend to do either.

"Hello," Hannah said, holding out her hand.

The woman just looked at it as if she'd offered her a dirty dishrag. She returned her gaze to Hannah's face, as if studying a specimen under a microscope. "You're young. Just what I thought."

Hannah let her hand fall. Obviously the woman wasn't in the mood to be courteous—or rather didn't know how to be. Obviously she didn't plan to introduce herself, so Hannah would just have to wait and see what would happen. She clasped her hands together and glanced at her expensive surroundings.

"If you're thirsty, you can help yourself."

"I'm fine, thank you."

"You know why I want to speak to you, but I hope you'll be patient with me."

"Of course," Hannah said, trying not to sound as confused as she felt. Who was she? Why did it matter? What did she want? The woman thought she knew her or should know her. Why? Then it clicked as the pieces fell into place. The woman now became familiar to her. She was Jade Walker's mother. She had shied away from photos recently—but the reason for it wasn't clear to

Hannah. Yes, the woman had aged, but she was still very attractive. Mrs. Walker had already started her tactical strategy against Amal. Hannah kept her features controlled so as not to appear amused.

"I think it's essential that a lawyer know all they should about their clients. It gives them the necessary information to defend them correctly."

The woman was arrogant and condescending. Hannah maintained her bright-eyed look of innocence. "Mrs. Walker—"

"You may call me Martha," she said, as if trying to make the meeting more informal. But it just put Hannah on guard.

"Martha, why would you want to help me?"

"Because you're young and inexperienced with a good future ahead of you, and I'd hate to see you fail."

"Thank you for your concern," Hannah said, trying not to choke on her words. "But I don't think we should be having this conversation, especially here."

A faint, humorless smile touched Martha's lips, and Hannah felt goose bumps race up her arms. "It's in your best interest that we do. Just listen and then you can leave. Are you sure you wouldn't want something to drink?"

"Yes," Hannah said, half expecting the woman to present her with a shiny red poisonous apple.

Martha tilted her head to the side, studying Hannah. "I know men so I think I know how Amal was able to manipulate you—"

"I wasn't manipulated."

"Convince you, then," Martha smoothly corrected, "to take his case." She shook her head before Hannah could contradict her. "As I've said, I know men. I know how their minds work. I've had four husbands, and I know how they operate. They can appear charming and fun, but mostly they are selfish creatures. My daughter discovered that with Amal, and you will, too. The only thing he is loyal to is his money and his mother. Have you met his mother yet? No? Then you will eventually. She's a ridiculous woman and a burden he should have disposed of long ago, but she keeps her claim on him and no woman can get past her. She's made sure of that, and he's weak enough to let her. He uses women for his own gains, but makes you feel as if you're the one who's failed him. And—"

Hannah held up her hand, her patience almost gone. She had to leave before her polite mask fell. "I truly appreciate you telling me this, but your bias against Amal is evident and—"

"My dear," Martha said with another one of her cold smiles, "I have no bias. Only facts. You don't want to fight this battle for him. When he was dating my daughter I saw all that you see now—the charm, the sex appeal, the brilliance. I treated him like a son and welcomed him into my family as one of us. I am not one to do that easily. My Jade was precious to me, and I thought she was with a man who would take care of her, but he destroyed her instead. He made her dependent on those pills due to his coldness, and there's a devious cruelty beneath that smile that I've seen. I hope you never do.

"I'm in a generous mood so I'll offer you two warnings. One, don't get involved with Amal Harper personally. You won't know the true pain of heartbreak until he's finished with you. And trust me, he will lose interest. He always does."

"And number two?" Hannah pressed when Martha paused.

"Drop his case. He will take you down with him, and I can assure you that I plan to take him down." She leaned forward, her tone filled with acid. "You don't want to be the one to stand in my way, because I will slaughter you—"

"I'm not easy to kill."

Martha chuckled. "Your naïveté is adorable."

"Thank you," Hannah said, taking it as a compliment although she knew it wasn't one.

"I'm giving you this opportunity to weigh your options. I know of an established firm that is looking for someone just like you. You'll rise faster than you could ever imagine. I have the connections to make that happen. I also know that your parents are facing some financial issues. I can make those problems disappear in the blink of an eye. All you have to do is walk away from this case." Martha shook her head. "No, don't say anything now. Think it over carefully. Decide whether you want to tie your life to a star or a rock. Whatever choice you make, you can be assured your life will never be the same."

Martha Walker's words echoed in Hannah's head as she dined in the cocktail lounge of a downtown hotel with her friends Natasha and Dana. They both thought she was taking a scary, unnecessary risk by taking Amal on as a client, but they wanted to celebrate anyway. It was a small crowd and the wine and food flowed, but Hannah barely noticed.

"Oh, my God, look at that woman," Natasha said, staring at someone near the far end of the room.

Dana looked, too, and frowned. "Someone should call her a cab and get her home."

Hannah turned to where her friends were staring and saw an attractive older woman fall out of her chair onto the ground. Hannah set her drink down and then started toward her.

Natasha grabbed her sleeve. "Where are you going?"

"She could be hurt."

"Or just drunk," Dana said.

"I'll be back in a minute."

"Let someone else handle it."

Hannah yanked her arm free. "I'll be right back." She rushed over to the woman, who looked to be in her fifties and was elegantly dressed. She smelled like expensive perfume and alcohol. "Are you all right?"

A waiter appeared at Hannah's side and shook his head as if he were watching a bad summer rerun. "She's fine, miss. Don't worry. We're used to dealing with her."

Hannah didn't like his tone or the look of disgust in his eyes. "I'll deal with her now. You don't need to worry anymore. Tell your manager that." The waiter hesitated and then left. Hannah returned her attention to the woman. A pathetic figure with her hair mussed up. "Ma'am, can I help you?"

The older woman glanced up at her with watery red eyes. "He was married. And all this time I thought he might be The One."

"Is there someone I can call for you?"

"I'm a stupid old woman." She covered her face. "I just want to die."

"No, you don't want to do that," Hannah said in a soft voice. "Come on, sit up. Let me call you a cab."

Natasha came up to her. "Hannah, leave her," she

said. "I heard the maître d' calling her son. You don't
need to get involved in this."

"I don't want to leave her by herself."

"There are a whole bunch of people here. You don't
have to babysit her. Prop her up on one of the couches
and—"

"Thanks, but I'm taking her outside," Hannah said,
ignoring the disgusted glances of the other patrons. The
woman deserved better than their scorn.

"Hannah!"

"Natasha, I'm sorry, but I have to do this." And she
did. She remembered when her father was learning to
walk again and how he'd tripped and fallen. People
just looked at him, making assumptions about the tall
African on the ground. They judged him without even
knowing his story. Hannah remembered the pride he
had being able to finally walk again without having to
use a walker to steady himself. She remembered hearing
strangers making comments that he probably couldn't
hold his liquor or that he was just a drunk. This woman
was someone's mother, and she needed protection and
Hannah would provide it. Sure, she didn't know why the
woman drank and she hoped she would stop one day,
but tonight she needed a friend and that would be Hannah. She knew how miserable she'd felt at the park until
The Stranger had arrived, and although she now knew
who he was, she'd never forget how he'd made her feel
that day. And she wanted to give that feeling of comfort and hope to someone else. To let the woman know
that even if for a moment she wasn't alone.

"Are you crazy?" Natasha asked.

"Are you thinking about the liabilities you're taking
on right now?" Dana queried.

"Yes, bye and thanks for the dinner. We'll talk later."

Hannah took the woman's slender hand and led her outside. The woman was surprisingly steady on her feet and leaned against the wall of the restaurant as though she hadn't been a tipsy drunk a few minutes ago.

"What's your name, dear?" she asked, her voice a little slurred but still clear.

"Hannah."

"A sweet name, like you. You can call me Doreen."

"Okay."

"Could you take me to this address?" she asked, handing Hannah a card. "I don't want to get a cab and I know they've probably called my son, and he just doesn't understand things. I don't want him to get mad." She lowered her voice. "I get scared when he's mad."

Hannah sensed true fear in the woman's voice. Was her son a monster? Was that why she drank? "All right. Come on." Hannah grabbed ahold of the woman's arm and walked a short distance behind the restaurant, and then helped the woman into her car. She jumped into the driver's seat and then looked at her new companion. She seemed to become more lucid as time passed, but she was still heavily influenced by something. Once they arrived at the address listed on the card, Hannah drove up to the guard at the gate. She was going to introduce herself when the guard glanced inside and pushed back his hat, revealing a big shiny forehead and thin brows. He released a long whistle. "Harper's going to blow a gasket when he sees her. How much has she had?"

"Enough." Harper? Was that her son's first name?

"Get her into bed fast. I can try stalling him for you if he comes through anytime soon," the guard said and then waved her through.

Once inside the gated community, Doreen led Hannah to her condo, and Hannah sighed. "You know, this is really dangerous letting a stranger help you like this."

"But you're not a stranger," Doreen said with surprise as innocent as a child's, making Hannah glad she was the person with her and not some scam artist. "You're a sweet young woman helping me escape my son's temper."

Hannah took the keys from Doreen, opened the front door and turned on the lights.

"Good," Doreen said with relief. "He's not home yet."

Get her into bed, that's what the guard had said, and then she could leave. "Let me take you to your room."

The condo was massive compared with the ones Hannah had seen. It had two levels, lots of windows and a gorgeous stone fireplace in the center of an immaculately furnished living room. Doreen led her to the left, where they entered her personal suite. She had her own bedroom, bathroom and kitchenette and an alcove.

Hannah helped Doreen change into a silk peach-colored nightdress that hadn't come off the rack in any store Hannah knew of. Her bedroom was palatial, with a large vanity mirror and decorations that suited a fairy princess. She helped Doreen into bed and tucked her in, relieved that her son would find her sleeping in her bed so that she'd be saved from his wrath. "Sweet dreams."

"I haven't paid you yet."

"Don't worry about it."

Suddenly, Doreen widened her eyes and gripped her sheets like a child instead of a woman in her fifth decade. "You'll stay for a while, won't you? There's some food in the fridge if you're hungry."

"Yes," Hannah lied to ease her worry. "I'll stay for a while. Now go to sleep."

"Good." Doreen rested her head back and closed her eyes.

Hannah turned to the door and then paused when her gaze fell on a framed photo sitting on the dresser. It was a photo of a little boy and a gorgeous man who looked vaguely familiar. The boy did, too. Hannah picked up the photo and studied it. The boy looked about seven. He stood smiling beside the big man at a barbecue.

"That's my son, Amal," Doreen said. "And his father. My ex."

Hannah nearly dropped the photo. Amal? Her son was named Amal? She quickly set the picture down. "I didn't mean to pry."

"It's the last photo of them together before my ex ran off."

Hannah edged toward the door, not wanting to know anymore. "I'd better go."

"You said you'd stay awhile." Doreen eagerly pointed to another photo on the dresser. "That's my Amal now. Isn't he handsome?"

"Yes." *And he knows it*, Hannah silently added. "Now go back to sleep."

"He's a good man."

"I'm sure he is," Hannah said just to be agreeable. Doreen was a changeable woman. At one moment she feared her son and the next moment she adored him.

Martha had called Amal's mother ridiculous, but Hannah found her rather sad. She could see him being devoted to her, but that was none of her business. She went to the door. "Good night," she said. She wanted to be gone before he came home.

"Night, dear," Doreen mumbled.

Hannah crept out of the room and gently closed the door. She was halfway down the hall when she heard the front door open and slam shut.

Chapter 6

"There's no use hiding, Mom," Amal said in a voice that could have woken everyone in the complex, fury filling every word. "I got a call from the restaurant and from Carl at the gate."

Hannah froze as the footsteps came closer, her heart seeming to beat at every pounding step.

"Did you think I wouldn't find out? I thought we'd agreed…" Amal came around the corner and then halted when he saw her. Rage turned to shock and then rage again. "What the hell are you doing here?"

"I—I—" Hannah stopped and lifted her chin, determined not to be scared of him. "I drove your mother home."

He took a menacing step forward. "You drove my mother home? You couldn't call a cab? Are you so hard up for cash you need to be a chauffeur, too?"

She took a step toward him, her eyes flashing. "Yes,

that's right. I saw this woman falling-down drunk in a restaurant," she said, satisfied when she saw Amal wince, indicating she'd hit her mark, "and I thought to myself, 'Yes, this would be a great way to make money instead of enjoying the cocktail party my friends had thrown for me.' I should've left her there on the ground so that everyone could've laughed at how pathetic and silly she looked. Besides, I didn't know she was your mother. I just felt sorry for her. Excuse me." She stormed past him.

He grabbed her arm. "I'm sorry."

Hannah sent a pointed glance to his hand on her arm, but he didn't let go. "Me, too."

"Where is she?"

"I just put her to bed."

He sighed and released her. "I'm sorry."

"I know. You just said that."

Amal softly swore and pushed past her.

Hannah spun around and followed him. "She's sleeping."

He swung the door open. "No, she's not. She only pretends to." He switched on the light and walked to the bed, turning down the photo of him with his father before standing in front of it. "Mom, what did you take, and don't play games with me."

His mother instantly sat up in bed, wide-awake, and flashed a beaming smile. "Oh, you're home. Hannah, have you met my son, A—"

"What did you take?" Amal interrupted.

Her smile faded. "I had one drink."

He folded his arms. "And?"

She wrung her hands. "Don't be angry."

"And?"

Doreen held up her thumb and forefinger. "And one tiny, teeny-weeny pill."

"You promised me you'd stop."

Her lower lips trembled. "He was married. I'd met him online and we'd been talking for weeks, and I finally get to meet him and he's married." She burst into tears.

Amal turned on his heel and left the room.

Hannah raced after him. "You can't just leave her there crying."

"She'll stop in a few seconds."

"Don't you care?"

"I've taught myself to stop." Amal walked into the foyer, reached into his jacket and pulled out his checkbook. "How much did she say she'd pay you?"

"I didn't do this for the money! No wonder she acts this way, having to live with such a cold, ruthless and heartless son. I'm not surprised she takes pills and drinks."

Amal's eyes darkened while his voice grew low and soft. "No, she does that because she doesn't want to face life. She wants life to be one big fairy tale, and when it isn't she resorts to drinking and taking pills." He pointed at Hannah. "I'm a good son and I've experienced more nights like this than you could ever know." He walked into the kitchen and rested his hands on the counter, his head held down. "There was the Middle Eastern tycoon who scammed her out of thirty-thousand dollars, the Dutch doctor who bilked her for forty, the handsome Greek who had two other women on the side." He lifted his head and stared at her. "But the best was the Nigerian prince who had lots of money but couldn't access it because of a major coup and just needed her bank account to transfer his funds into. My mother lost a total of over one hundred thousand dollars before I was made aware of the dealings she had entered into with this unscrupulous thief. Oh, but you would already know something about that, right?"

Hannah gritted her teeth at the barb but didn't reply. She was well aware of what was called a 419 Nigerian scam. The 419 scams worked by gaining a person's trust and, through skillful social marketing techniques, bilking naive individuals, like his mother, into believing they were helping and would make more money if they just provided some of the investment funding. But she wouldn't be provoked.

"You can think of me any way you want at the office, in the park, but my home is off-limits to you or anyone. So don't you dare come into my private space and judge me when you know nothing."

"I know you like broken women."

"What?"

"Is that what attracted you to Jade? You thought you could save her?"

"You're my lawyer, not my psychologist."

"And maybe not even that," Hannah said in a light tone, glad to be able to catch him off guard.

"What do you mean?"

"I had an interesting chat about you with Martha Walker. She made me a very tempting offer."

"And will you take it?"

"That depends on you."

Amal folded his arms. "What do you want?"

"Respect would be nice. A thank-you would be even better instead of accusations of being a mercenary or some Nigerian scam artist."

He sighed. "Thank you, Hannah."

"You're welcome." She headed for the door.

"Watch out for the Walkers. They have claws."

She opened the door. "Says the man with a large pair of his own."

Amal kicked the door. He shouldn't have lost his temper, and now he could lose her. He'd never had to apologize this much to one person, but he knew he needed to—he just didn't know why. Amal wasn't afraid of many things, but the prospect of losing Hannah scared him. He dashed out the door and ran after her as she marched to the elevators. "Hannah, wait." For one brief moment he thought she'd keep walking and ignore him, but she stopped and slowly turned.

"Look," he said. "I'm sorry about everything— especially the Nigerian scam artist thing. That was stupid of me to say." He stopped when he reached for her, and she recoiled from his touch. That was a first for him. Women never did that. But he had no business touching her anyway, and he couldn't understand his desire to. He rubbed the back of his neck and then shoved his hands in his pockets, looking like a schoolboy caught breaking a window with his baseball. "I need you to understand something."

"Yes?" Hannah said, pursing her lips. He found the motion distracting because soon he was focusing on her mouth. Her beautiful mouth painted a nice purple hue that made him think of grapes. Ripe, juicy, sweet grapes…

"Amal?"

He jerked back to attention. "Huh?"

"You were about to explain something…."

"Yes." He cleared his throat. "About my mother."

"You don't need to explain her to me."

"Yes, I do. I don't want anyone judging my mother or me or my relationship with her. It's more complicated than at first glance. I know she appears like some old, rich kook, but she's not. Given the chance she can be bright and funny and—"

"I know," Hannah cut in with a fierceness that surprised him. "I didn't judge her. When I saw her all I wanted to do was help."

Amal tilted his head, curious. "And when you found out she was my mother?"

"Honestly?"

He nodded.

"I swore."

He laughed. "At me or her?"

"At myself."

"That's a safe answer."

"I know."

"At least let me give you something to drink before you go."

Hannah rested a hand on her hip. "And if I say no?"

"Why would you say no?"

"I have a lot of reasons."

"How about I give you a reason to say yes."

"And that would be?"

"With me you'll never have to wonder what you're missing, and I'm great company when I choose to be."

Hannah gestured toward the hall. "Lead the way."

"You're not going to argue?"

"It's been a long night. Consider yourself lucky."

"I do."

Moments later they both sat at stools against the large island in his kitchen with two glasses of red wine.

"You look very lovely this evening," he said.

"You just noticed?"

"No," he said in a low voice, making his admiration clear.

"I was celebrating with friends." She tapped the stem of her glass. "See, I've got this fabulous, lucrative new case, but the problem is my client."

Amal raised his eyebrows in exaggerated curiosity. "And what's wrong with your client?"

"He's a bit too arrogant for my taste." She took a sip of her wine and then set it down. "He likes to be in control, and he can be deceitful."

"Does he have any good points?"

"I'm still searching."

He winced. "Ouch."

"I do like how he cares for his mother."

He lowered his gaze. "So he's a mama's boy."

"No, it's more complicated than that. But I understand it."

He met her gaze, searching. "You do?"

"I remember when I was in elementary school I used to cringe when my mother would come to pick me up."

"Why?"

"Because most times she'd call me by my Yoruba name and her accent at the time was so thick people couldn't understand her. Sometimes I'd catch my friends giggling at certain words she said. What was worse was when she knew I was embarrassed—it nearly broke my heart. She asked me if I was ashamed of her, and I lied. But at the time, I was, because I so desperately wanted to fit in. I didn't want jollof rice and okra in my lunchbox. I wanted peanut butter and jelly sandwiches just like everyone else. But I had to learn that she was my mother, though I hid her away as I got older. I took rides from friends instead of having one of my parents pick me up. Because, like you, I didn't want anyone to judge them, and I could see in strangers' eyes how they saw them—as African immigrants and the stereotypes that go with that. They didn't know that in Nigeria my mother had been a homemaker and my father a government worker who both studied, but in the United States she became a preschool teacher and he a construction worker."

"Those are still fine careers."

"But not the same."

"No."

Hannah glanced at her watch and stood. "I should be going."

Amal didn't want her to go. He wanted her to stay the night so he could kiss her again and slowly peel away the black dress she wore and find out if her bra unlatched from the back or the front.

Amal walked her to the door, hating every step that brought her closer to leaving him. "Thanks again for what you did."

She winked. "You can add it to my fee."

Amal followed her into the hallway. "So you're still my lawyer?" he asked, trying to sound casual although he could feel his chest tighten.

"For now." She pushed the elevator button. "But I'm still considering my options."

"When will you decide permanently?"

She shrugged. "I'll let you know."

Amal flexed his fingers to keep them from forming into a fist. "You have two days."

"I prefer four." The elevator door opened and she stepped inside.

"Three."

She turned to him, a slow smile spreading on her face, her brown eyes bright with mischief. She wiggled four fingers as the elevator door slowly closed.

Amal rested his head against it. He had it bad. He wanted her as his lawyer and as his woman, and that definitely wasn't going to happen. He couldn't let it. He banged the door with his head. He had to snap out of it. He had to remain distant and professional. A partner and a colleague, nothing more. He straightened, taking a deep breath and feeling more in control. He turned and glanced down and saw an earring. One of Hannah's loop earrings must have fallen out. He picked it up. It suited her. Elegant with a bit of flair. He held the earring gently in the palm of his hand, knowing it was costume jewelry but not caring. He wondered if she liked dancing, concerts or dinner cruises. What was her favorite dish? He closed the earring in his fist. It didn't matter. He'd never know. He shoved the earring into his trouser pocket and returned to his condo.

"Oh, has she left already?" his mother asked while meeting him in the foyer. She looked refreshed from the shower she had taken, as if the nightmare of the evening hadn't happened.

"Yes." He clicked the door shut, resisting the urge to slam it. *Four days.* He had to wait four days for Hannah's reply.

"Oh, that's a shame. Did you get her number?"

"What?"

"You'd better have because she's perfect for you. You must have noticed."

"Mom—"

"She's beautiful, smart, caring and—"

He rested against the door and shook his head. "Do you have any idea who that woman was?"

"Yes, I told you. Her name is Hannah, but I didn't get a last name. That's your job. I hope you got her full name and number and scheduled a date. She's wonderful and just the type you need."

"I told you I'm not—"

"Forget about not dating right now. You can't miss this opportunity. I even made her stay so that you'd get a chance to meet her. A woman like that doesn't come in a man's life every day."

"She's also my lawyer."

Doreen shook her head. "No, she's not."

"Yes, she is."

Doreen frowned. "But that can't be right. That pretty little girl—"

"She's not a little girl."

"—can't be the one you hired to beat the Walkers. She'll get swallowed up."

"She's tougher than she looks."

"She's younger than you. How much experience has she had?"

"That doesn't mean she can't win."

"But—"

Amal squeezed his eyes shut. "Mom, you're missing the point." He stared at her. "Of all the women in the world, you had to have one of your episodes with *her*."

"Amal…I'm so sorry. I never would have guessed. I

knew you were desperate for representation, but I didn't expect you to go get a young, inexperienced…"

Amal held up his hand and shook his head, his voice low and steady. "Underestimate her at your peril." He pushed himself from the door and walked to the kitchen, hating the restless feeling assailing him. "But you know what? It's good that you see her that way. It gives her the advantage and she knows how to use it."

"You've seen her in action?"

"I can imagine." Yes, he could imagine a lot about her, but nothing that he could say aloud.

"She has a great figure," Doreen said, as if reading his mind.

Amal felt his face grow warm. His mother knew him too well. "It doesn't matter. I need her to see me in a certain light—as strong and in control, and tonight I wasn't. She may reconsider representing me."

Doreen's face fell. "Because of me?"

He knew he couldn't blame his mother for this. The Walker case was his fault, not hers, and he'd lost his temper with Hannah, not her. If Hannah decided to take the Walkers up on their offer, he didn't have the leverage to stop her. He hadn't given her a reason to stay. "No," he said with regret. "Because of me."

He deserved better. Hannah sat on the park bench and absently watched a group of kids playing soccer. She hadn't slept well last night, not just because she'd lost one of her favorite pair of earrings, but because she couldn't stop thinking about Amal. He deserved better representation than her. He deserved someone who wasn't conflicted about his character. Someone who dealt with facts and not emotions. She wanted to be neutral but couldn't be. One moment he could make her temper ignite and then just as easily charm it away. If she took the Walkers up on their offer, she wouldn't have to deal with her mixed-up feelings and everything would turn out all right because she'd still get the money she needed for repairing her parents' house.

But then Amal wouldn't have anyone. But maybe no one was better than someone who had doubts. It was unfair to lie to him about her belief in him. She knew the portrait Martha had painted of him as a ruthless businessman and mama's boy was an exaggeration, but she also knew there was a seed of truth. There were sides to him she knew she hadn't seen. She didn't trust herself or her intentions. And yet she knew that Martha's intentions were far from pure and her dark side was likely more vicious than his. But what did Martha really want? Did she really want to offer Hannah a warning, or was there something she was afraid of?

If Martha expected to win, why did she need to make threats? There was something more to the story, but Hannah knew finding it out could mean a nasty battle—one she could fail at.

But she didn't like to fail, and she knew Amal didn't, either. She may have muddled feelings for Amal, but she was certain that she didn't trust or like Martha Walker. She would stick by him. He was her right choice. Martha may consider herself a star and Amal a rock, but Hannah knew a star could burn bright and then fade away, while a rock could last for centuries. She'd tie her dreams to a rock and see where it would take her.

It had been two days since he'd heard from Hannah, and he was already slowly going crazy. Amal adjusted the setting on his stationary bike for a steeper incline and stronger resistance. He needed to work out his frustration. He was glad the gym wasn't too crowded although it was late afternoon. He wiped some sweat from dripping into his eyes. This wasn't like him. He didn't wait on anyone. He should be looking for alternatives. He should be the one in control—making her dance to his tune. But the awful fact was he didn't want a replacement. He wanted her.

"Why am I not surprised to find you here?" Hector said, leaning on the empty bike next to Amal's. "What's up?"

"The Walkers got to Hannah."

Hector's mouth fell open. "What? That fast? Bonnie didn't tell me that."

Amal frowned at him. "Who's Bonnie?"

"Hannah's assistant. We've been seeing each other."

"Since when?"

"It's a casual thing. Relax. Tell me about Hannah."

"Like I said, the Walkers got to her."

"And she took the bait?"

"She's thinking about it."

"Then what are you doing here? You should be at her place changing her mind."

"She has four days to decide."

Hector nodded. "Ah...you gave her a deadline to put on the pressure and let her know that you don't need her."

No. She set the deadline to let me know she doesn't need me. "Something like that."

"What are you going to do now?"

Amal stopped pedaling and rested against the handlebars. "Go home. She has two more days."

"Shouldn't you offer her something more?"

"I'm not going to beg." Even though he was close to wanting to.

"Will you be able to make it today?"

"No," Amal said, remembering the family picnic Hector had invited him to.

"We'll miss having you."

"Another time."

Hector patted him on the back. "Talk to you Monday then?"

"Yes," Amal said, heading for the locker room. He should wait two more days, but he couldn't. He had to see her.

Chapter 7

Hannah wasn't surprised when Amal walked into her office that Friday afternoon. She'd been expecting him. She knew he wasn't a man who liked to be kept waiting. However, Hannah was surprised by how happy she was to see him. "How can I help you?"

He sat down and placed an object on her desk. "I wanted to return this."

Hannah smiled at the sight of her lost earring. "Oh,, good, you found it. Thank you." She reached for it.

He moved it out of reach. "You can thank me another way."

"How?"

"By giving me your answer."

"I have two more days to consider."

Amal shook his head. "You don't need that long to decide. You're a quick thinker, and by the expression on your face I bet you've already made up your mind."

"Would you like to guess what it is?"

"No, I'd like you to tell me."

She folded her arms.

He turned away. "You have a nice office."

Hannah studied him, wondering what his next tactic would be. "It's a work in progress."

He sat. "When Jade and I were first starting out we could only afford a little hole-in-the-wall. In the winters we froze and in the summers we roasted, but it was a beginning and we were too happy to care. Slowly, our business grew and we were able to move out, but I'll never forget where I started."

"A touching story. Does it have a point?"

He looked at her. "A lot of great things can come out of humble beginnings. Jade knew that. She didn't use her parents' money to get the company started, and she could have. She knew that if she did that somehow they'd own it—and her. She didn't want them involved in her life or anything she built. She wanted an identity separate from them because she knew that taking Walker money comes with a high price."

Hannah nodded. "Food for thought." She leaned back. "If you've found another lawyer, that's fine with me."

"That's not why I'm here."

Hannah leaned forward. "Then why are you here?"

"I told you why."

"And I told you that you are two days early. See, when I make an agreement with someone I stick with it. You can't just come in here and waste my time because you have nothing better to do."

He stood. "I didn't—"

She stood, too. "When I say four days, I mean four

days. You may be able to change the rules with the people you work with, but not with me. And if I'm going to be your representation, you'll have to get used to how I work. If I say I'm going to do something on a certain day, I'll do it no later, no sooner. So you can guess what my answer is, but you're not going to hear it for another two days. Is that clear?"

Amal waited. "So what's your answer?"

"I just told you, you'll have to wait."

He snatched the earring as she reached for it. "Then you don't need this."

"You're being childish."

He raised a mocking eyebrow.

She sighed. "We had an agreed deadline."

"No, you made an arbitrary deadline that you want me to follow."

"You just don't like not being the one in control."

Amal glanced down at her earring. "Said the pot to the kettle."

"Fine." Hannah held out her hand. "Let's do a simple exchange. You first."

He handed her the earring.

"I'm surprised you didn't argue," she said, repeating the statement he'd given her the other day.

"I'm too tired. What's your answer?"

She stood and came around the desk. "No."

Amal jumped to his feet, furious. "No?"

Hannah gently pushed him back down. "Just listen."

He stood. "What do you mean by 'no'?"

"Sit down and I'll tell you."

"I don't want to sit down."

"Look, you don't need a lawyer."

"What do you mean I don't need a lawyer?"

She covered his mouth. "Let me finish. Okay?"

He narrowed his eyes.

"Nod once and I'll remove my hand."

Amal briefly shut his eyes and then met her steady gaze and nodded.

"Good." Hannah removed her hand. "I'm still going to help you. I've done a lot of thinking, and the Walkers are hiding something. We're going to find out what it is. So this is the deal. You fix my parents' place and I'll get the Walkers for you."

"I don't need you to 'get them.' I need you to—"

"What you need is someone to find out why the Walkers are running scared and threatening people so that they won't represent you. It makes no sense. I know that once I uncover what they are really worried about you'll get your inventory and the Walkers will never trouble you again."

"Okay," Amal said, slowly trying to process everything. "So what exactly is our relationship then?"

"I'm your consultant. I want them to think you're alone and failing, and then we can catch them unprepared and swoop in."

Amal was quiet a long moment and then said softly, "So you're no longer my lawyer?"

"No."

"Good."

Hannah frowned, confused by the sudden relief on his face. "Good? A few minutes ago you looked like you wanted to wring my neck."

"But I think your idea is perfect. Do you like Italian?"

"Yes. Why?"

"Because I want to take you out for dinner."

"For business?"

"Absolutely not. Pleasure will be the only thing on the menu."

"Really? I thought I wasn't your type."

"I lied. In case you haven't noticed, I like you a lot."

Hannah shook her head and sighed. "Amal—"

"How about a movie?"

"No."

"A sports game of your choice?"

"No."

"The theater? The symphony? A museum? A trip to the Caribbean? Am I getting close?"

"I just don't think we should—"

"I know," he said quickly. "I agree. I really don't think we should get involved, but no matter what I think I can't help how I feel and I can't stop myself from wanting you. And I've tried. It doesn't help that my mother hasn't stopped begging me to ask you out, so if not for me, saying yes would make an old woman happy."

"Your mother isn't old."

He shrugged. "Can I get a tiny yes?"

"This is emotional blackmail."

He nodded. "Is it working?"

She grinned. "Yes."

Amal punched his fist into his palm. "Excellent. What will it be?"

"Coffee."

His face fell. "Coffee? You want me to take you to get coffee? But that's so boring."

"I like coffee, and we might as well get this over and done with. I'm not as exciting as you think."

"Yes, you are. Fine. You'll get coffee. I'll pick you up Sunday."

"Why don't we just go out now?"

"You'll have to wait for Sunday."

She rolled her eyes. "Fine. You win. Besides, I'm beat. I'm ready to go home, so you can walk me to my car."

"You're a thrill a minute."

Hannah laughed as she grabbed her things. She waved at Bonnie's shocked expression as she left with him. She knew she'd have a lot to answer for later. They flirted on the way to the parking garage, and most of Hannah's apprehension of saying yes had disappeared. She was about to agree to going to a movie when she saw a familiar figure disappear around the corner. He moved fast, but not fast enough for her not to recognize him: he was Martha's man. The one who had told her to get in the limo. He was watching her, and she knew that her decision not to represent Amal the way they expected was a good choice. Now she had to make it look convincing. She had to put her plan into action without giving Amal any warning. Hopefully he would either catch on or forgive her.

Hannah spun to Amal and said in a loud voice. "Didn't I tell you to stop following me?"

Amal stopped. "What?"

"I'm not going to represent you. I'm not going to be your lawyer."

"There's no need to shout when I'm standing only two feet away from you. And I know that, but I thought—"

"You thought wrong," she rudely cut in, marching to her car. "Go find somebody else to take your case. It's not going to be me."

Amal lightly touched her sleeve. "But you said—"

Hannah yanked her arm away as if he had an infectious disease. "You don't need to tell me what I said. I know what I said. Now I need you to listen. I'm not going to be taken in by your charms, and besides, this case is a loser, so stop wasting my time." She opened her car door. "Excuse me."

She was about to get into the driver's seat, but she made the mistake of looking at him first. He appeared devastated and for a moment she almost relented and told him it was just an act, but when she caught a glimpse of Martha's man peeking his head around the corner, she knew it was for Amal's own good. She'd hoped to have ignited Amal's temper, that he'd narrow his eyes and call her filthy names. But instead he just stood there as if she'd stabbed him. So she turned away and got into her car and closed the door. She turned on the ignition and then drove out of the lot. In her rearview mirror she saw the familiar figure jump into his own car and drive away.

Hannah wanted to do the same but couldn't. She made a U-turn and returned to the parking garage, hoping she could catch up with Amal before he was out of sight. But she didn't have to worry. He hadn't moved. He was standing in the same spot where she'd left him. She drove up to him and lowered the window on the passenger's side.

"Get in the car," she said.

He didn't move.

"Amal. I said get in the car."

"What just happened?"

"Get in the car and I'll tell you."

He folded his arms.

"Please. This is important."

Amal got in and slammed the car door closed.

"I'm sorry. I saw an opportunity and I had to take it."

"What opportunity?"

"I just saw Martha's assistant spying on us, and I wanted to give him a juicy story to tell her."

"I think you succeeded."

"You have a right to be angry, but…"

"But what?" he snapped. "You could have given me a warning. A signal or something."

"It was impulsive. I thought you'd just get angry with me and…"

"I was too stunned to be angry."

"But you're angry now."

Amal glared out the window.

"Do you want to shout at me?"

"No."

"Why didn't you get mad at me?"

"I don't know."

"Yes, you do."

"Because of the plate," he said in a voice too low for her to hear.

"What?"

He turned to her. "I'd just come back from a local fair with my dad. We'd had one of those great father-and-son days people like to talk about, and to my shock he asked me to help him clean the prized plates he'd received from winning fishing tournaments. I was never allowed to touch them, so this was a big honor for me. I helped him for over an hour, but then as I was replacing one…" His voice faded away.

"You dropped it?"

Amal closed his eyes and nodded. "In an instant that day was ruined because of me. My dad went from happy to furious in one second, and it was my fault. I was always ruining things for him." What he didn't share was the sight of his father's face—the revulsion and the words that followed. "You're an imbecile like your mother. I give you something simple to do and you screw it up. You're always screwing things up. I wish I'd never asked you to help me. I should have known better, so maybe some of your idiocy is my fault. Now clean it up."

"I'm sure that wasn't true," Hannah said, lightly touching his hand.

"It was." Amal sighed, trying to push the pain of the memory away, but it lingered.

"Well, if he told you that, then he's a bastard."

Amal turned to her, shocked. "No, no, it wasn't like that. My father was well respected. Everyone loved him. Only I could make him angry. And I—"

"You were a kid. Accidents happen. He should have just given you a lesson about being more careful and left it at that. He had no right to make you feel guilty."

Amal shook his head. "No, you don't understand…"

"No, you don't. You're never the reason for someone else's fury—especially when you're a kid. The rage was already there and you were just the unfortunate target. Maybe someone cut him off while driving or gave him the finger or maybe he had a bad day at work or something. But his anger at you was extreme and not your fault at all. And if he made you think it was your fault, he lied to you."

"Look, you don't know my father—"

"No," Hannah shot back. "But I know you. And I expected you to fight for yourself, to get angry at me.

To tell me how you felt. But you crumbled. You looked at me as if I'd betrayed you."

"It was just that, for a moment, when you were shouting at me, it took me back there to that day. I couldn't get angry, because I just wanted to know what I'd done wrong so that I could make it right again."

Hannah sighed, exasperated, and started the car. "That's just the point. You didn't do anything wrong. Not today or back then. So you broke a plate. That didn't mean you were a bad son." She grabbed his hand and squeezed it. "I promise I'll never switch on you like that again."

He forced a smile. "Thanks." He glanced around. "Where are we going?"

"I thought I'd treat you to some ice cream."

"I don't want ice cream."

"Then what do you want?"

He sent her a significant glance. "That's a dangerous question to ask a man."

"Is it?"

"Yes."

"Well, I can't give you *that* right now."

"You could pull over to the side and we could try."

"And be charged with indecent exposure."

"I've never been caught."

"Another time."

"You promise?"

"Let's change the subject." She drummed her fingers on the steering wheel and then hit it as an idea came to her. "Oh, I know what you'll like."

"What?"

She winked. "Trust me."

Chapter 8

Hannah took him paddleboating at Mountain View State Park.

Amal was surprised at first but then got the hang of things. He'd never done anything like that before. They spent time casually paddling around the lake.

"I didn't expect you to think about this. And I certainly didn't think I would enjoy myself. This was a good idea. What made you think of it?"

"I don't know. I just saw people paddling and I've never taken the time to do it, so I thought it'd be something fun to try."

"So, you're having your first time with me?"

"I'm not going to answer that."

Amal smiled. "You just did." He stopped paddling and reached for her hand.

Hannah moved it away. "What are you doing?"

"Enjoying myself. Come on, give me your hand."

"We're supposed to be paddling."

"We're in a lake, going around in a huge circle. We're essentially going to end up right where we started, so what's the rush? Relax and enjoy yourself." He reached over and took her hand.

Hannah was silent a moment and then said, "I think the Walkers…"

Amal shook his head. "No talk of work."

"I'm really sorry about—"

He shook his head again. "I don't want to talk about that, either."

"Then what do you want to talk about?"

"Nothing." He patted her hand and then closed his eyes and tilted his face toward the sun.

Hannah watched him, wondering what he was thinking and envying his calm. They had a lot to do and think about.

Amal gently squeezed her hand. "Stop thinking so much."

"How do you do it?"

He looked at her. "Do what?"

"Just sit there."

"Easy. When I'm at work, I work. When I'm away, I play. Nothing else matters. I learned it a while back when I used to run track. Running made me forget my troubles at home. You should try it."

"Running?"

"No, forgetting your troubles. Don't think about the Walkers or your family. Just enjoy this moment."

Hannah failed at first. She couldn't stop herself from thinking about what she had to do, but soon she let her mind wander. She looked around the pond and focused on a squirrel taking a drink before disappearing under

a bush. Then her attention went to an older man and a young girl tossing a ball. Yes, this was nice. It had its own special magic. She and Amal sat in the boat holding hands and enjoying the day until the early-evening sun touched the water with a golden ray of light.

After returning the paddleboat they had started to walk toward the car when Amal abruptly stopped.

"What's that?" he asked.

Hannah turned to him, surprised. "What's what?"

He sniffed the air. "Don't you smell that?"

Hannah did the same and noticed the scent of grilled chicken and Latin spices. "Yes, someone's grilling."

"Mmm… Doesn't it smell good?"

"Yes." Hannah looked around and then found the source and pointed to a large crowd over to the side. "Looks like they're having a party."

He walked toward them. "Let's join them."

She grabbed his arm. "But we don't know them."

"They don't need to know that," Amal said and then tucked her arm through his.

Hannah pulled away. "I'm not crashing somebody's party."

"Fine, then I will."

Hannah followed him, frantic to find a reason to stop him. "It's too risky. You're a businessman. What if you're caught? What about your reputation?"

"Who's going to report me? No one'll recognize me."

"Maybe you haven't noticed, but they're all Latino," Hannah said. "You'll stand out."

"There are black Latinos."

"I know, but…" She seized his arm again. "You'll fit in, but I won't. You're able to charm anyone."

"If you act the part, you are the part. Watch me."

Amal slipped out of her grasp before she could stop him. He walked up to the crowd and smiled and then grabbed a plate and started filling it. Hannah felt her heart leap into her throat when she saw a couple talking and staring at him. The man was large and muscular with a long ponytail and tattoo on his arm. The woman also had a tattoo, though she looked less fierce. Hannah swallowed hard, wondering if she should run over and warn Amal, but it was too late. The big man walked over to him and started talking. Amal nodded and then spoke, and the man hugged him. Then the woman came over and hugged him, too, and then became animated. What lie had he told for them to welcome him so warmly? Hannah edged closer just to hear what story he was telling.

Amal gestured her over, but Hannah shook her head. There was no way she was going to do something that bold. She watched, stunned, when he started to dance with one of the older women. His ease with the group showed another example of how different they were. She wasn't surprised when soon his dance partners were two young women. He was definitely in his realm, not hers. She turned and headed for her car. She wouldn't force him to stop his fun. He could call a taxi home.

"Wait!"

She turned and saw a girl of about nine running up to her. She grabbed Hannah's hand. "Come on."

"I don't—"

"It's okay. Uncle Amal said that you were shy and I had to look after you for him."

"Uncle Amal?"

"Yes, and he said you're Auntie Hannah." She led

her to the picnic table loaded with food and grabbed a paper plate. "Here you go."

Hannah took the plate and started to fill it, wondering what story he'd told them about her. Perhaps he'd told the girl she was his sister, though they looked nothing alike. She glanced at Amal dancing with the two ladies. No one would dare assume that he and she were a couple, she thought sourly.

The girl caught Hannah's look and smiled. "Uncle Amal loves to party."

"Especially with pretty women."

"The prettier the better," the girl said, as if repeating an often-uttered phrase.

"Maybe he'll meet his bride that way."

She giggled. "No way. Uncle Amal doesn't like marriage."

"Oh, he told you that?"

"Everybody knows that."

"Everybody?"

"Yes."

Before Hannah could ask any more questions, the tattooed couple Hannah had seen before came over and greeted her. "We're so happy you could join us," the man said.

"Thank you," Hannah stammered, again amazed by their warmth. What story had he spun for them to believe that they belonged here?

"So are you and Amal...?" The woman let her words fade away so that Hannah could fill in the blanks.

"Sort of," she said, not sure of what story he may have given them.

"I have you to thank for bringing him here."

Hannah sat at one of the tables and started eating

and then saw Bonnie. She blinked to make sure. *Bonnie* was here? Bonnie's eyes widened when she saw Hannah. She rushed over to her.

"What are you doing here?" they said in unison.

"You first," Hannah said.

"I'm here with Hector. His cousin hosts this family gathering every year, and it's been ages since Amal's come. How did you manage it?"

She hadn't. Amal had played a trick on her. He hadn't crashed a stranger's party. "Excuse me."

Hannah went to the dance floor and politely cut in. When Amal pulled her into a dancer's embrace, she said, "You snake."

He smiled.

"You tricked me."

His smile grew.

"You knew this was Hector's family and made me think they were strangers."

"I wanted to see what you would do."

"You have a devious mind."

"It made the night more interesting, right?"

The musician playing a guitar sported a conservative haircut and hippie mustache. He stopped playing for a moment and talked to the crowd as he switched instruments.

"We probably should get going," Hannah said, glancing at her watch.

"What's the rush?" Amal said, taking her hand. "It won't take long to listen for a little while."

They walked up to the musician, who'd been singing a mixture of salsa, calypso, jazz and Afro-Latin. He looked at the crowd.

"Hey, I could use a little help with my next number," he said. "Anybody interested?"

Amal held up his hand and pointed to Hannah. "She is."

Hannah turned to him, stunned. "What?"

The musician smiled. "Just what I was looking for, a pretty lady by my side."

Hannah waved her hands and shook her head. "But I don't—"

"Just pick up that tambourine and follow my lead."

"Yes, follow his lead," Amal said and then shoved her forward.

Hannah glared at him while the others in the crowd encouraged her to join the musician. Reluctantly, she picked up the tambourine. At first she felt awkward but then she got into the rhythm of things, adding her own flair and moves. Soon she was singing along, and the crowd was, too. She got people cheering for another song, and that attracted an even larger crowd. After nearly half an hour, Hannah took her bow and left the makeshift stage.

"You should come back," the musician said. "I could use a lady like you to spice up things."

"No," Hannah said with a shaky laugh, surprised she'd become so bold. "This was a onetime event."

Amal rested his arm on her shoulder in a possessive gesture. "And she was only on loan."

The musician nodded. "I hear you, brother."

Amal lead her away.

"What do you mean 'on loan'?" Hannah demanded.

"I didn't want him getting any ideas, and fortunately he understood me. That's all that matters."

Hannah shook her head in disbelief. "Men. I'll never fully understand you."

He squeezed her close and kissed her forehead. "But you like us anyway. Especially me."

She playfully hit him in the chest. "I'm not sure about that. How did you know I could play the tambourine?"

"I didn't. I just wanted to see what you would do. You're a woman of hidden talents, and I plan to discover them all." He bent his head and pressed his mouth against hers.

Far from being like the kiss of before, this one was warm, wet and searching. His lips traveled from her mouth and then slowly slid down her neck and landed on her shoulder.

"We can't do this here." Hannah groaned when she felt the teasing tip of his tongue on her skin.

"No one is watching," he said in a deep, sly voice.

"If you keep this up, they'll start to."

"But I've been waiting days to do this." His gaze lowered to her blouse. "Minutes to do this." He removed the top button on her blouse. "Seconds to do this." He let his finger trail a sensuous path from the base of her throat to her chest.

She grabbed his hand before he could go farther. "We have to stop this."

"No, we don't." He glanced up and then gestured to something in the distance. "There are some bushes."

"I'm not doing 'it' in the bushes."

"Where's your sense of adventure?"

"It's not there, that's for sure."

"It could be fun." A slow smile spread on his face. "I'll make sure of it."

"No." She pushed him away, suddenly angry. "I'm

not ready for that yet, and if that's all you want from me then let's stop right now."

He frowned, confused. "No, that's not all I want. Why would you think that?"

"Because that's what you do. You seduce women. That's what you're known for. I mean, within minutes you had two women dancing on you like honeybees."

"That's a strange analogy."

"You know what I'm trying to say."

He furrowed his eyebrows. "Not really."

"I know you're a great lover, but—"

"How do you know?"

"There are rumors."

Amal rested a hand on his chest. "I'm flattered but wouldn't you prefer to know from experience rather than gossip?"

"And be added to a long list?"

He threw up his hands, annoyed. "Oh, so that's what this is all about? You think I'm the 'love them and leave them' type."

"You can't deny your reputation."

"Do you know how long I was with Jade?"

"Two and a half years. A record for you. There were even rumors that you'd actually get married, but we know that will never happen."

"I was true to her, truer than many husbands I've met."

"She's the only one who had that benefit."

"I've never cheated on anyone. I admit at times I've dated casually…"

"Sometimes two or three at a time."

"It was never a secret. If I'm with a woman exclusively, she knows she's the only one."

"Until you get bored. I'm not going to be one of your rebound ladies. I thought we could simply go out as friends and…"

"As friends?" His voice cracked. "Do you usually kiss your friends like that?"

"Amal, I—"

"Or let them hold you that close. You feel what I feel." He clenched his teeth and his eyes darkened. "You can try to pretend it's not there, but it won't go away. And I'm not on the rebound. I told you those rumors about me are exaggerated, but if you want to believe them, that's fine. I don't need this. I'll talk to you about the strategy on Monday." He turned and pulled out his phone.

"Where are you going?" Hannah asked.

"To get a taxi."

Hannah watched him go, wishing she could feel some sort of victory. But she felt sadness instead. She had gotten him to stop his carefree, playboy ways and see her as an individual. She'd had a great time with him, and she didn't want it to end like this. She didn't want her time with him to end at all. He was right. She did feel what he felt, and it felt marvelous. She ran after him. "I'm scared, all right?"

He stopped but didn't turn. "Scared of what?"

"How you make me feel. You make me do things I'd never do on my own. I'd never pick up a tambourine and play it in front of a bunch of strangers. I'd never impulsively go paddleboating. With you I'm impulsive and a little reckless, and it scares me. It scares me how much I enjoy being with you when I'm not really sure why you're with me." She held up her hand before he could reply. "Yes, I know you want sex, but after that what else?"

"Wow." He slowly turned to her, amazed. "You're able to compliment and insult a man at the same time." He sighed and shook his head in pity. "You're a strange one, Hannah. Do you really think I only want to sleep with you? Wait, don't answer that, because you'll make me angry, and I don't want to be angry."

"Look, I know what you're like and—"

He pressed his finger against her mouth. "No, you don't. You think you do, but you're wrong, and I'm going to prove it to you." He took her hand and led her to her car.

"How?"

"What are you planning on doing tomorrow?"

"Well, I have some errands and—"

"Okay, I'll help you do your errands and then take you out for lunch, and I won't mention sex once. I won't hint at it or anything."

"Okay," Hannah said, curious if he could meet the challenge. She smiled, feeling suddenly buoyant. She looked forward to spending another day with him.

"Are you sure?" Martha asked with eagerness when Peter told her what he'd witnessed that afternoon.

"Yes, she won't represent him."

"How did he take it?"

"Not well. He looked dejected. I've never seen him like that. He didn't even argue."

Martha rubbed her hands in triumph, feeling almost giddy. "We have him just where we want him. I knew that girl had sense. Now there's nowhere else for Amal to turn. He'll have to come crawling to us, and we'll set the terms and watch his business completely topple." She walked over to the large painting of Jade on her living room wall. Her secret was safe. Amal would never learn of it, and everything would stay as it was meant to.

"I'm in the mood for some champagne," she said.

"What are you celebrating?" her husband, Granville Thompson, asked as he entered the room. He was her fourth. He was a distinguished man in his seventies who treated her with the reverence she wanted. He didn't mind being in the shadow of her family name and at times being referred to as Mr. Walker. Her name represented power, and he knew she wouldn't change it for anyone less powerful.

"The Amal situation is coming to a close."

"You're still working on that? Just give the poor boy what he wants and put an end to it. You're making more of a mess than necessary."

"I don't make messes. I clean them up."

He took a seat. "I told you in the beginning you were getting into trouble."

"I'm not in trouble," Martha bristled, annoyed by his criticism. "I just told you. The situation is coming to a close."

"I don't think he'll give up as easy as you think."

"Are you on my side or his?"

"I just think that you're going about this all wrong."

"Everything that was Jade's belongs to me. Us. This family. The inventory. I won't allow him any part of it."

"Even if it's a part of him?"

She knew very well what her husband was talking about, but she refused to acknowledge it. The thought scared her. She couldn't have Amal close. She knew that he could take away something else that she treasured, and she wouldn't let him do that. Losing Jade had nearly destroyed her. Losing what she was protecting would make life not worth living. She knew her husband, as a man, couldn't understand this protection that she had for her secret. But she would defend it no matter what. For Jade and herself she would win this battle.

Her husband came up to her and lightly touched her shoulder. She found his touch reassuring, but she still felt a shiver of fear inside that what he said was true. That Amal may not stop. But she chose to believe what Peter had told her. She'd gotten to Hannah, and she would get to anyone else he tried to use against them. She was used to winning and she refused to lose.

She gazed at the beautiful oil portrait of her daughter and made a silent vow that although she'd failed her in life, she would not fail her in death.

She touched her husband's hand and then looked at Peter. "Get that champagne. It's time to celebrate."

Hannah half expected Amal not to show up the next day, but he surprised her and was ready to go. First they went grocery shopping at one of her favorite stores, which carried a selection of exports from the West Indies and Africa. Then she took him to the post office, where they stood in a long line, but he waited patiently. He didn't seem to mind that nothing exciting was happening, and soon she just enjoyed his company. For lunch, he took her to a nice little restaurant in a trendy part of town, where they chatted, not about business but about things that interested them. She learned that he enjoyed going to the gym, that he once bicycled across three states and that he once owned a pet rabbit. Hannah shared stories about her debating days in college, how hard it had been after her father's accident and why she wanted to become a lawyer and how disappointed her family had been.

Quickly, she regretted the conditions of her time with him. There was no intimacy, not even a faint hint. She wanted him to reach across the table and touch her hand and then maybe play footsie with him under the table. She wanted to feel the sensation of his fingers skating across her arm. She wanted to face her fears and conquer them. She wanted to see him as he truly was, and not what she needed him to be or what others said he was. She didn't want to see him through the filter of Martha's words or what the tabloids said. She wanted to be with him.

She wanted to brush away her own biases. From the start she had been unfair to him by just seeing him as a playboy when he really was different from any other man she'd ever known. He was the first to just listen to her and hear what she had to say. She stared at him from across the table, and at that moment he was the stranger she remembered from that day in the park. The one she'd dreamed about night after night, the one who had given her the buttercup she kept in her diary. The one who made her feel as though she could do anything. She got a tiny thrill knowing that he did want her, because she wanted him, too, and she wouldn't let that scare her. Most of her life she felt she had to just focus on work so that she wouldn't be distracted, but for the first time it was nice to have someone in her corner, to know that she wasn't alone. She realized that with him that's how it could be.

She started to reach for his hand, ready to tell him how her feelings had changed, when a voice cut through the air.

Chapter 9

"Amal? Who is she?"

Hannah glanced up to see an attractive young woman glaring at her, trembling like an agitated wasp.

"Evie, not now," Amal said in a neutral tone. Not angry or frustrated, just eerily neutral. "We'll talk about this later."

"No, we'll talk about this now. Who is she?"

"She is none of your business."

Evie turned her venomous glance to Hannah. "Do you know that we were going to get married? Do you know the promises he made to me? The hopes and dreams this man gave me and then took away?"

"This is just a business meeting," Hannah said in a cool tone, ignoring Amal's sharp stare. "I'm sorry if there has been any misunderstanding. I have no interest in him as a man, so if you want him you can have him."

Her face brightened. "Really? This is just a business meeting?"

"No," Amal said.

"Yes," Hannah said.

Evie furrowed her eyebrows. "Which is it, yes or no?"

Amal stood and said, "Excuse us," and then he took Evie's arm and led her outside. Hannah watched their body language through the restaurant window. Surprisingly, Amal kept his gestures controlled, but she could still sense the anger. Then Evie's face crumbled and he hugged her. Hannah began to grin. It was clear Amal was good with distressed women, but her grin turned to a look of horror when she saw Jacob walk past and then stop and look at her. She tried to cover her face with her hand, but he'd already spotted her. He waved and then walked inside the restaurant.

"What a surprise to see you here," he said with a bright smile.

"This is not a good time," Hannah said, sending a glance toward Amal, who was still consoling Evie. She needed to get rid of Jacob before he returned. "I can't talk right now. Call me later."

He sat. "I just want to congratulate you about the good news regarding your parents' house. Your mother told me the roofing has been fixed and the plumbing, too, and now they're working on the electrical. Amazing how fast things are getting done."

Hannah stared at him, amazed. She didn't know that. How could the work on the house have already started when she'd talked to Amal only yesterday about working with him?

"Are you, sure?"

"Yes," he frowned, confused. "You didn't know?"

Abigail hadn't told her anything. "Oh, I've just been

so busy I've lost track of time," Hannah said in a light voice so that Jacob wouldn't suspect anything. "I am so glad the house is being taken care of." She glanced up and saw Amal coming toward the table. "And I really must stop this discussion because I have a lot to do today."

Jacob leaned forward, concerned. "You seem tense. What's wrong?"

Amal approached the table, his tone terse but polite. "You're in my chair."

Jacob jumped up and held out his hand. "I'm Jacob Omole."

"Amal Harper," Amal said, shaking his hand and then claiming his seat and turning his back on him.

"So how do you know Hannah?" Jacob asked.

"Jacob, not now," Hannah said in a pleading voice.

Amal turned to him. "How do you know her?"

"We used to date."

Amal nodded. "I have a couple of exes myself."

"More than a couple from what I've heard," Jacob said.

Hannah stood, took Jacob's arm and whispered, "This is a business meeting—a very important one. If you ruin this for me, I'll never talk to you again."

"It's only a business meeting?"

"No," Amal said.

"Yes," Hannah countered. "Now go."

He shot Amal a look and then looked back at Hannah again. She made a shooing motion with her hand. He shook his head and grabbed another seat, placing it at the table. "You're not going to care, but I have to say this. Hannah's a wonderful woman and has plenty of people who care about her. If you hurt her in any way,

I know people who will make your life miserable." He took Hannah's hand and kissed it. "You'll always be in my heart."

"Jacob, it's not like that."

He flashed one of his special grins as he got up. "Don't worry, I won't tell your mother." He held her hand a moment and then turned and left, and she knew it was for good.

Hannah fell back into her chair, trying to regain her composure.

"Why do you keep telling people this is a business meeting?" Amal asked.

"Because it makes things easier."

"For whom?"

"Evie won't be threatened by me and Jacob won't be threatened by you."

"Why shouldn't they be? I told Evie it's over, and I'm sure you told Jake—"

"Jacob."

"Whatever," Amal said with little interest. "He already saw through your story. I don't think lying to them helps matters."

"I didn't want him telling my parents about—" She stopped and finished her salad.

"About me?" he pressed.

"Don't take it personally. It's complicated."

"I'd like to meet your parents."

"You will. Just not yet."

"Why not?"

"Because it's too soon."

"You met my mother."

"That's different. She doesn't think we're serious."

"We're not?" he asked, surprised. "I thought we

were. I just spent time doing boring tasks with you because I like you. If that's not serious, I don't know what is."

"Not marriage serious."

He sat back as if she'd struck him. "It's a little soon to talk about marriage."

She laughed at his unease. "Relax. I know you're not ready for marriage and neither am I, but my family thinks I should be and everyone is looking for Jacob's replacement. I don't want you to have that kind of pressure."

"Don't worry about me. I can take pressure, and most people like me. I'm good with parents."

"Yes, that's another thing." Hannah set her fork down and folded her arms. "Jacob just told me that work is already being done on my parents' house, but I didn't agree to help you until yesterday."

Amal glanced at his plate. "Hmm."

She kicked him.

"Ow!" He rubbed his shin and glared at her. "What was that for?"

"What are you not telling me?"

"Nothing."

She kicked him again.

"Ow!" He narrowed his eyes. "Stop that."

"Then stop lying. You're behind the work on their house, aren't you? How did you find out where they lived? How did you know all that needed to be done?" She paused as a thought came to her. "Oh, yes, your friend. The one whose number you gave me. He told you, right?"

"I thought you didn't have time to waste."

"How would I have afforded it if I hadn't decided

to work with you? Was this a preemptive strike so that I'd be forced to—"

"You have a nasty mind, you know that? I just wanted to help you. It had nothing to do with the case. When my friend told me how bad things were, I wanted to help you and…" He stopped and then suddenly laughed.

"What's so funny?"

His eyes danced with humor. "We're more alike than we'd like to admit."

She frowned, annoyed. "How so?"

"I remember being suspicious of you when you helped my mother, and now you're suspicious of me helping your parents. I guess when it comes to our families we're very guarded and find it hard to trust people. But from now on, let's start."

Hannah shook her head. "But the repairs costs thousands and thousands of dollars, and you're in a legal battle and—"

"And I never want to see you cry again like the way you did in the park." He took her hand in his. "Hannah, I'm a nice guy. I did it because I wanted to and I could. I'm not flush with cash, but I still have a lot more than you do. Just accept it for what it is. A gift."

It was hard for her to do so. It was hard for her to believe that her parents' troubles were really over and that she wouldn't be able to repay him in the same way. "What happens if I can't find out what the Walkers are hiding?"

"Doesn't matter."

But it would matter to her. She couldn't be indebted to him like this. She didn't dare let herself believe that he could be this wonderful that he could really have fixed up her parents' place at all cost to him because he cared about her that much. He could get any woman he wanted. Ones with far less drama in their lives than she had. Why would he have done something so amazing with no thought of return? Was this really who he was? Was he the kind of man who didn't mind lazy weekends just shopping and going to lunch? Not just partying and late-night carousing? Was he really the kind of man who took charge of problems that overwhelmed her? Someone she could trust?

He said he wanted to prove who he really was to remove her prejudices about him, and this did just that. Or was it another type of seduction? Seducing her with his contacts and money?

Amal released her hand and sighed as if reading her thoughts. "I can't have you thinking the worst of me every time I do something nice."

"It's not that." It was, but Hannah knew she had to conquer her fears. She couldn't keep second-guessing herself or him. She had to find out what he was really about, and one way to do that was to give him what they both wanted and deal with the consequences later. "Let's do it tonight."

"Let's do what?" he asked, cutting through his fish.

She glanced around the restaurant and then lowered her voice. "It."

He lost grip of his knife and it skidded across the table. "But you said—"

She waved her hand impatiently. "Forget what I said. Let's do this. Come to my place around seven."

He reached for his knife and absently set it on his plate. "You're serious about this?"

"Yes."

"What changed your mind?"

"Does it matter?"

"Yes," Amal said with force. "If there's a chance you'll change it again."

"I won't." She stood. "Let's go."

Amal called over the waiter for the check. "Why now?"

She put her lips close to his ear and whispered, "I have to do a few things to prepare. Don't you want me to be completely ready?"

Amal grinned and didn't say another word.

Tonight was going to be one to remember. Amal emerged from his shower whistling. At last the mystery of Hannah Olaniyi would be solved. He could just picture her sprawled out naked on her bed, ready and willing. He was fully lost in his fantasy when his phone rang. He glanced at the number and then answered.

"Now's not a good time," he said to Hector.

"There's a problem."

He opened his closet and shuffled through his shirts. "Handle it. I'm busy."

"It's your mother."

He selected a shirt and laid it on his bed. "What about her?"

"She's had another episode."

Chapter 10

Hannah stared at her wardrobe. What should she wear? Did it even matter? In a few minutes she wouldn't be wearing anything anyway. She wanted this. She was ready for this moment and didn't want anything to ruin it. Especially herself. She put on her sexiest underwear and then a simple dress. Something easy to pull on and off.

She set the stage in her bedroom—changing the sheets to the four-hundred-thread-count selection. She covered the lampshade with a light red cloth and then debated about spritzing the sheets with a subtle floral perfume, but she ultimately decided against it. She glanced at her setup, pleased with herself, and then went into the kitchen, where she had cheese and crackers arranged on a plate. She glanced at her watch. He should be there in minutes.

When the doorbell rang, she took one final look in the mirror before answering the door.

Bonnie stood there with a bottle of wine. "I thought you could help me open this. But from the look of disappointment on your face, I guess you were expecting someone else."

"Yes, but it's still good to see you," Hannah said, not wanting her friend to feel bad.

"But if it's Amal, you're going to be disappointed."

"What do you mean?"

"He's not coming. I guess my evening was ruined for the same reason yours is. I was with Hector enjoying—"

Hannah shook her head. "I don't need details."

"Dinner and a movie," Bonnie finished with a smug grin. "Then he gets this call and his face changes. He gets up and leaves the room and then apologizes and says he has to do something for Amal and rushes out."

Hannah sighed, glancing at her clock again. Amal should have been there by now. Whatever had happened had stopped their evening together. She opened the door wider. "Come in. No reason for that bottle to go to waste."

The two women sat in Hannah's living room with the platter of cheese and crackers and enjoyed the wine. "So how is the case progressing?" Bonnie asked.

"There isn't going to be a case." She'd left her folders at the office but knew this was a good time to discuss her suspicions. "The Walkers are hiding something, and once we uncover what that is I think Amal will get what he wants without needing a lawyer."

"What could they be hiding?"

"I want you to find all you can about the Walkers' assistant, Peter Lawford. He's been following me and I want to know why."

"What will you do?"

"I'm going to find out why Martha has been hiding herself recently. She used to be seen at most social events but stopped several months ago."

"When her daughter died."

"Yes, but for someone so social, why such a drastic change? She went through three nasty divorces, and that didn't stop her. Neither did the death of a beloved brother. But when her daughter dies, she secludes herself and wants to take what Amal owns—stuff that's relatively peanuts compared with what they have. That's what I have to discover."

"Well, I'll do whatever I can, boss."

They spent the next hour discussing their strategies, and then the phone rang.

Bonnie looked at it. "Aren't you going to answer it?"

Hannah shook her head. "Let him leave a message. I don't feel like talking right now." *Or hearing excuses, even if they're good ones.*

"Too bad." Bonnie snatched the phone off the table. "Hi, yes, she's here," she said as Hannah gestured for her to tell him she was out. "Just a minute." She covered the receiver. "Be nice and listen to him. He sounds upset, and if you'd seen Hector's face you'd know it's something bad."

"Okay," Hannah said, feeling a little ashamed of her pettiness. She was saddened, but she was sure he was, too. She took the phone, and Bonnie gave her a thumbs-up for luck. Hannah stuck out her tongue, making her laugh. "Hi. I know you can't make it."

"Yes, I'm sorry about this," Amal said in a distracted rush. "Rain check?"

"Only if you'll tell me what happened."

He fell quiet and then she heard him sigh.

"Amal?" she said, her curiosity and concern growing.

"It's nothing."

"Hold on." Hannah looked at Bonnie. "I need to take this in another room," she said and then left and went to her bedroom and closed the door. "Is it your mother?" When he didn't reply she pressed him. "Amal. It's me. Tell me what's wrong."

"Yes, it's Mom. It's bad this time. The police were involved. I convinced them not to charge her with disorderly conduct."

"I'm sorry."

"Me, too. More than you could ever know," he said with such a feeling of regret and disappointment in his voice. "What are you wearing?"

Hannah paused, surprised by the question. "I'm sorry?"

"I need a distraction. Tell me what you're wearing right now."

"A dress."

"Come on. You can do better than that. Is it long or short? Does it have straps or sleeves?"

"You really want to know?"

"I wouldn't ask if I didn't."

Hannah looked down at her dress. There wasn't much to say about it. "It's short and lilac colored."

"What about underneath it?"

"Well," Hannah said in a teasing tone, "since I was going to meet you, I didn't think I needed to worry about that."

Amal swore and groaned. "You're not wearing anything?"

"Just kidding. I'm not that brazen."

"You'll learn."

"I'm wearing a lace panty set."

"I bet you it's white."

"And if it is?"

"Damn."

"But it has a thin red trim."

"Where?"

"All over."

"Hmm."

"I'd better go."

"Hannah," he said quickly. "It's not always going to be like this."

"I know. These things happen."

"I'll make it up to you."

"I'm counting on it. Bye." She hung up. They were stopped before anything even started. Hannah stared at the phone. He'd tried to maintain a playful tone, but he sounded really strained and worried, so she couldn't really be angry with him. Instead, she'd be there for him.

Amal gripped the phone receiver in two hands and pressed it against his forehead, reminding himself to count to ten. Hannah understood and she forgave him, but that didn't make him feel any better, because he'd lied to her. He'd told Hannah it wouldn't always be like this, but that wasn't true. This was the reality of his life. Calls from the police, calls from restaurant managers, calls from associates—always about what his mother had done. Jade had also had to deal with his mother's antics before slipping into her own troubles. He partly wondered if the stress of his mother had pushed her toward using and abusing prescription pills.

"Don't be angry with me, Amal," Doreen said, coming into the main living room. As a functioning drunk her words were barely slurred and her walk steady.

Amal set the phone down, pleased with his control. "You're supposed to be asleep."

"I'm sorry, baby."

He squeezed his eyes shut, wishing he could block out her voice. "You're always sorry."

"I don't know what happened."

He stared at her, taking a deep breath to keep his temper under rein. "What happened was that you drank too much again and got violent."

"I just wanted to be left alone and that woman at the bar—"

"I don't want to hear it because I don't care."

"I didn't do it on purpose. I don't know what comes over me."

"You need to stop drinking."

"I don't have a problem with drinking. I can stop anytime, and I have. You know that. I'm not an alcoholic. Even the clinic said so."

Yes, the clinic and the doctors all said she wasn't an alcoholic, just that she was destructive. Her psychiatrist at the rehab had warned him that once she was off the pills she'd take to something else. She'd told him that his mother possibly had an addictive personality and liked to create chaos. She suggested that his mother take up a hobby like knitting. His mother didn't even know how to thread a needle. Neither of them were good at simple hobbies. Like him, she liked the external thrill of nightlife. Going out was her hobby, and he didn't know how to stop her or if he even could.

"Mom, why do you do this?"

"It was just a bad night. That's all. I like to drink, that's all. I had a problem with pills, but I—"

Amal shook his head, stood and began to pace. "I don't know if I'm doing you any good by having you here."

She gasped. "Amal, you wouldn't."

He saw the look of fear on her face. No, he could never kick her out. He couldn't abandon her the way his father had. He was all she had and she depended on him. No matter what she did, she was his mother and he loved her. He had to protect her—from herself. He softened his tone. "I'm not kicking you out. I just want the best for you, so I'm just thinking aloud."

"Don't talk about things like that. This is my home. My place is with you, and I'm improving."

That was his fear—he was afraid she wasn't. Her episodes were erratic. He could never guess what would set her off. Recently, she'd become more unpredictable since his fight with the Walkers. Maybe the stress was too much. "Mom, I think you need a vacation."

"No, I'm okay. I think I'll go to bed now."

It was her way of shutting him out, and he knew he wouldn't be able to reach her anymore tonight. "Good night." He watched her head down the hall toward her suite, and then he returned to the couch. Tonight was supposed to be special. A dream where he made love to a beautiful woman who made him smile. Instead, it had become a nightmare, forcing him to face a monster with an addiction he could not slay.

Amal fell asleep on the couch. He woke up to the scent of coconut oil and humming. He pried his eyes open and saw a female form sitting in front of him. Hannah was in a dress with her hair pulled back, showing her dangling earrings. She had a soft smile on her face. He shut his eyes again and then paused. *Hannah?* His eyes flew open—it was Hannah. He scrambled up into a sitting position and rubbed his eyes to make sure he wasn't dreaming. "What's going on? What are you doing here? How did you get in here?"

She held out her hand. "Relax."

How could he relax when his heart was racing? He was excited, stunned and wary all at the same time. He didn't know if he should hug her or shake her hand. He gripped the couch cushions instead. "Are you really here?"

"Yes."

He wanted to touch her to make sure she was real. He wanted to pull her into his arms and let her know how much he was glad she was there. He gripped the cushions tighter instead. "Who let you in?"

"Your mother. Don't worry. She's in her bedroom. She just finished a hearty breakfast."

"It's morning?"

She nodded.

Amal covered his face and inwardly groaned as he felt the night growth on his face. Then he glanced down at his crumpled shirt and trousers. He must look like a bum. This was not how he wanted her to see him, but he didn't want her to leave, either. He had to relax and take control. "You look great."

"You look like hell."

He grinned. "I feel like hell."

"Go take a shower. That will refresh you. Then we can have breakfast."

"That's a good idea." He stood and took her hand. "Come on."

She resisted. "You don't need me."

"I thought we could shower together."

"I don't—I can't."

"Why not?" He winked. "You can scrub my back for me."

"But we're not lovers. At least not yet. I know we were going to be, but we didn't."

Amal shook his head, confused. "I don't follow."

"We're not close enough to shower together yet."

He folded his arms. "Are you saying because we haven't slept together I can't see you naked in the shower?"

"First you become lovers and then everything else follows. Those are the rules."

"There aren't any rules. And if there were I don't play by them anyway. Come on."

Hannah pulled her hand away. "No. I can't."

"Fine." He glanced at his watch. "Let me clean up and then let's do it now."

"No."

He rested his hands on her shoulders. "Hannah, it's just a shower."

"With both of us naked."

"I know." His mouth spread into a wide grin. "That's the best part."

"But what if you change your mind?"

"About what?" he asked, exasperated.

"About sleeping with me."

"Why would I do that?"

"Look, lovemaking is different. It's under sheets, in the dark."

"Sometimes."

"With the lights down low then."

"Sometimes."

Hannah folded her arms, determined. "You've been with a lot of women and I don't want to be compared. Not in that way."

"The only woman who matters to me is you." He held up his hands in surrender. "But okay, I won't take this relationship any faster than you feel comfortable with. We'll shower after we've slept together."

"Thank you."

"Of course there's another option."

"What?"

"I could make love to you in the shower."

"How would that work?"

"Use your imagination."

"No."

"You don't know what you're missing. I'll file that away for later."

Hannah shoved him toward his bedroom. "Go take your shower."

"I can't change your mind?"

"No."

Amal sighed. "I'll be back in a few. Promise you won't leave."

"I promise."

He dashed into his bathroom and quickly showered and shaved. He whistled his way into his bedroom and then halted when he saw Hannah in his bed, her eyes poking out from beneath the covers. He crossed the room with a grin. "Ah, yes. This is a nice touch." He kneeled on the bed and then pulled the sheets away. His face fell as if someone had popped his balloon. "What is this?"

"What do you mean?"

"It's like opening a Christmas present and finding a lump of coal."

"What are you talking about?"

He gestured to her dress. "You're supposed to be naked."

"I thought you'd want to undress me."

Amal bit back a laugh at her outrage. "All right. Turn around."

Hannah sat up and folded her arms. "Not if you're going to make it sound like a chore."

Amal turned her back to him and unzipped her dress. "My God, you have your bra and panties on, too?"

"I thought foreplay was the fun part."

"What the hell is foreplay?"

Hannah jumped up and spun around to him. "Foreplay is—" She stopped when she saw his mouth quirk. "Are you laughing at me?"

"No." He bit his lip, but his eyes were bright with amusement.

"I'm glad you find this so funny." She turned and marched to the door.

He grabbed the back of her dress. "You're not going anywhere."

"Yes, I am."

He swept her in his arms. "You're right. You're going to bed." He set her down on the sheets. "And we're going to make love." He pushed her dress from her shoulders. "And you're going to enjoy it." He pressed his lips against her bare skin. "In that order."

"Not if you're going to make fun of me."

"I'm sorry, but when you mentioned foreplay like we were supposed to follow *The Ladies' Guide to Sex* I nearly lost it. But I'll be serious now. I won't tease you anymore." He pushed her dress to the ground. "Do you have any requests?"

"Requests?"

"Would you prefer me to remove your bra or panties first?"

"You decide."

"Okay. You remove your bra and I'll remove your panties."

Hannah nodded. "Should we do it on the count of three or something?"

Amal choked back a laugh. "No."

"You're making fun of me again."

"I'm not," Amal said, but when she looked at him he burst into laughter.

"I don't see what's so funny."

Amal held his sides and kept laughing.

"Now I'm leaving." Hannah reached for her dress.

Amal quickly sobered. "I'm sorry. Really. I didn't mean to laugh. It's just that, don't you know how to have any fun? You're too formal about this. It's supposed to be relaxing. There are no rules when it comes to this."

"That's not true. There are certain acts that are illegal in some states—"

He shrugged. "Who's going to know?"

Her eyes widened. "But—"

He shook his head. "Stop being a lawyer for once and just let things happen." He unhooked her bra and then slowly slid her straps away. "I want you to relax and be comfortable with me."

"Like this?" She draped her arms on his shoulder and then licked the bottom of his chin.

Amal cleared his throat, shocked by her bold move,

his Adam's apple bobbing up and down. "Yes, that's good," he said in a hoarse voice.

"Let's turn off the lights," she whispered.

"The lights stay on."

"But we're supposed to set a mood."

He rolled his eyes. "Baby, I'm already in the mood." He tossed off his clothes and stood before her, his arms outstretched. "If you haven't figured that out by now, I don't know what will convince you."

Hannah cleared her throat. "Yes, I just—"

He covered her mouth with his. "Hmm…yes, that's better."

He removed her bra and then her panties, and his hands skimmed her form while his eyes trailed the length of her with mounting desire. "You're so beautiful."

Hannah fought not to think of all the other women he may have said the same words to. She watched him roll on a condom, wanting to stay in the moment and enjoy it. Enjoy the feel of his touch that triggered primitive yearnings, igniting her hunger for him. She arched her body into him greedily, wanting to feel his hot flesh all over her. She nestled into his supple strength, caressing him gently with her fingers. She loved the feel of him. She loved the smell of him. She loved him.

It was an overwhelming admission but one she couldn't deny. She'd fallen in love with him, and it was too late to turn back. She met the full force of his passion with an equal force of her own. She wanted to make him hers. She wanted to erase from his mind every woman he'd ever been with. She wanted to be the only one who ever knew the white-hot release of having him inside her, the liquid fire of his mouth as it slid across her skin.

She let go her inhibitions, the rules, the rituals and all that she thought she was supposed to be. She let the wild desire that filled her take over. She taunted his nipples with her tongue, licked the inside of his thigh and delved into his mouth while also opening herself up and welcoming him inside. She felt the drumbeat of his heart and playfully slapped his bottom. "You're mine now," she said, knowing he'd never comprehend what she really meant.

"Oh, yes," he breathed, his breath hot against her chest. "And you're mine."

Always, she silently said. "I'm going to get the Walkers for you."

"Don't mention them right now."

"But I'm making you a promise."

"I don't need that kind of promise."

"But—"

"No business talk," he said and then effectively stopped her for the next hour.

Once they were through, Amal lay staring up at the ceiling in amazement. He couldn't stop grinning. Hannah had a wild side he hadn't imagined and couldn't forget. He wanted to be with her again and again and again. Next time it would be at her place and then maybe the beach and…

The sound of the smoke detector interrupted his fantasy.

Chapter 11

"What is that?" Hannah asked.

He swore, knowing exactly what it was. He shot out of bed, grabbed his robe and raced into the kitchen, where he saw his mother waving away smoke from the oven. He disconnected the alarm and opened a window. He spun around and sent his mother a withering look.

"Hannah told me you had a hearty breakfast. So what did you need to cook?"

"I was just trying to reheat this bread," she said in a soft voice.

"Then use the microwave. We've been over this. You can't cook."

"I didn't want to disturb you. Oh—hi, Hannah."

Amal didn't turn to Hannah because he didn't want to see the look on her face. She'd been exposed enough to his mother's behavior, and he wouldn't blame her for wanting to distance herself from him.

"You should go," he said.

"Only if you want me to."

He turned to her, moved by both her words and her tone. It was soft and understanding, and he felt his tension ebb. She didn't judge him or his mother. It was going to be okay.

"Doreen," Hannah said. "What are your plans for today?"

"Oh, I don't know. My friend Lorraine invited me for Scrabble."

"That sounds like fun. Let me help you get ready."

Amal watched them go and then cleared up the mess. Moments later his mother emerged, looking bright and happy. "Well, I guess I'm ready to go."

Amal plastered a smile on his face. "Have fun."

She waved and then left.

Hannah looked at him, concerned. "Should she go by herself?"

"It's okay. Her friend is only two floors down and she'll be gone all day."

"For a game of Scrabble?"

He laughed at her innocence. "They don't play Scrabble. They order takeout and watch dirty movies."

"Oh."

"Sometimes they'll order a male stripper. They have a favorite they call 'The Officer.'"

"You're making this up."

He shook his head.

"Well, your mother is definitely an interesting woman."

"Want some cereal?" Amal asked, in no mood to prepare anything more complicated than that.

"No, I'm fine." He prepared his breakfast and then

sat at the kitchen table. He wanted to thank her for staying and understanding everything, but instead he scooped up his cereal and ate in silence, delighting in the crunching sound. He imagined he was grinding out every problem in his life.

Hannah sat in front of him and studied him for a moment and then said, "You're not the reason your mother drinks, you know. I am."

He stared at her. "What do you mean?"

"Your mother isn't that drunk. She just plays the part so that she can get attention. She's afraid of losing you."

Amal set his spoon down and tapped his chest. "But she's the one who wants me to date."

"A part of her does, but a part of her is afraid of being replaced in your life, and this is the only way she knows how to be noticed by you. I mean, besides bailing her out of trouble, what do you two do together?"

He picked up his spoon again. "Nothing. She has her life and I have mine."

"I bet you that if you took her out every once in a while these episodes would disappear. She's scared, that's all."

"But that sounds so childish," he grumbled.

"I know, but after your father left, what happened?"

"She fell apart so I had to take care of her."

"And that's the only relationship she knows—you taking care of her. She thinks that's the only way to keep you in her life. You'll have to show her a different way."

"How?"

"Take her out to dinner and talk to her about her day. Listen to what she has to say. Don't scold her. Just listen and give her a new kind of attention. Then she'll change."

"I don't know."

"Just give it a try."

"Come with us."

"No, this is between you and her."

"No, this has been between her and every woman I've had in my life. Now that I think about it, you're right. Her episodes always got worse when I was either in a relationship or distracted by business."

"See?"

"That's why you need to be there, so that she'll know nothing will replace her."

"Okay. Set a date and I will."

The Walkers were good at keeping secrets and better at convincing others to keep their mouths shut. Even though Hannah was polite and tried to be subtle, nobody at the country club, the horseback riding school or the boutique where Martha frequented would say anything about her, good or bad. Even friends of the latest "Mr. Walker," husband number four, kept mum. It was expected, but after three weeks of false starts Hannah was starting to get nervous. Bonnie also had little success finding out anything about Peter Lawford.

"He's like a ghost," Bonnie said as they ate lunch in Hannah's office. Half-eaten cartons of Mexican takeout sat on the table. "He has an almost nonexistent digital trail, which is an amazing feat in this day and age. He's from Chicago and worked in the food industry briefly as a taster, but that's about it before joining the Walkers three months ago."

"How did they find out about him?"

"He was signed with an employment agency. Exclusive. I have a meeting to speak with the director tomorrow. Not sure I'll get much, but I'll try."

"Thanks. You're doing better than I am."

"What do you have?"

"Right now? Nothing. I'm not worthy of being spoken to. I'm obviously from the wrong circles."

Bonnie began to grin. "Then use someone who is from the right one."

Hannah returned her grin, knowing whom she meant. "Yes, Natasha. I'll get her to do a little digging for me."

"And I have an aunt who owns an exclusive nail salon where Mrs. Walker likes to go. I'll get you an appointment."

"You're the best."

"I know."

Hannah picked up the phone and then dialed her friend. "Hi, Natasha. I need a favor."

Natasha reported back several days later. She came to Hannah's office, trying to pout but failing. "You know I'm still mad at you about your cocktail party."

"But you love me anyway."

Natasha smiled. "Anyway. I didn't get much, but I did find out that Mrs. Walker had started filling several new prescriptions."

"Is she ill?"

"That's the strange part. She looks very healthy, but suddenly she had been ordering more prescriptions and making frequent doctor's visits. But no one knew why."

"I know her daughter had a prescription drug addiction. Maybe she was supporting her habit and trying to find a new way to treat her before she died."

"Could be, but why do everything under her name?" Natasha asked.

Hannah shook her head. "I don't know."

"I did find out something about Jade."

"What?"

"She was taking diet pills. Everyone I spoke to told me how upset Martha was about her daughter's weight gain and how she had made a big performance about taking her to the gym and giving her diet pills. She blamed Amal for her daughter eating loads of food. Two plates full. Before she passed away she was a big girl. There were few pictures of her because the Walkers were really protective. She didn't take the breakup with Amal well. She became an overeater."

"Are you sure?"

"Yes, and I was able to get proof." Natasha took out her phone and showed Hannah an image of a large woman finishing off a pizza. "This was taken at a charity event in New York with a camera phone. That's why it looks fuzzy, but that's how Jade looked before her mother completely hid her away."

"But it can't be," Hannah said in awe and dismay. "She's close to a hundred pounds overweight."

"Try seventy-four. She joked about it with one of the guests. I sent the image to you so you can show Amal."

Hannah bit her lip. "I'm not sure I should. This isn't the woman he would remember."

"But it would explain why the Walkers are out to get him."

Medication? Diet pills? Did that sound like Jade? It was possible that she replaced one addiction with another. "This is good, thanks."

"I tried to be as subtle as I could, but you better find

something quick before the Walkers find out that you're onto them. I don't think you have much time."

"Medications?" Amal said when Hannah asked him about Martha's health. It was late evening and they'd just finished dinner. They lay on her couch, watching TV. "No, I don't remember her ever taking anything other than herbal supplements."

"I can't seem to put the right picture together about her. She's a new recluse, visiting doctors and taking medication. Maybe she's dying."

"But then why hold on to vital inventory to spite me? This is personal."

"Yes," Hannah said, wishing she didn't have to bring up the second topic. "The coroner's report said that Jade died of heart failure, right?"

He nodded. "From an overdose."

"So they said. I now wonder about that, though. It's possible she did it to herself because she was depressed over you, and that's why the Walkers blame you."

"What do you mean?"

"It seems that Jade gained a lot of weight after you broke up."

"That's impossible. Jade was never a big eater. She hardly ever had an appetite."

"Well, suddenly she did and her mother had her taking diet pills and keeping her out of the public eye. It seems she'd gained over seventy pounds."

Amal shook his head. "No, she wouldn't. My jewel wouldn't do that. She was always slender. Gaining weight was hard for her."

Hannah inwardly cringed at his reference to Jade as his "jewel" when he had no special name for her, but she knew he deserved the truth. She showed him the picture she'd printed off her computer so that he could study it closely.

He took one glance at it and looked away. "No, that's not her."

She waved the picture at him. "It is. Look closely."

His jaw twitched and he folded his arms. "No, Jade wouldn't do that to herself. Not because of me, not because of anybody." He stood and pointed to the picture. "It's not her. It's someone else. You've made a mistake."

"It was confirmed. This was her before the Walkers took her out of the public eye."

Amal firmly shook his head. "No."

Hannah stood and held the picture up to his face. "Don't be so shallow. The woman you loved is there. Okay, so she's not slim and she's wolfing down a pizza, but she's still there. Look at her face. Her eyes. Her mouth. This is her."

Amal snatched the picture and sank into the seat. "No, I…" His words fell away as he studied the image. "I did this to her?" he said, his voice cracking with pain.

"No, she did this to herself, but perhaps the Walkers blame you for this."

"I tried to help her. Why didn't she call me?" He looked at Hannah, searching for answers she couldn't give him. "I wouldn't have let her do this."

"She was a grown woman. She made her choice."

"Do you think this is the secret they are trying to keep?" Amal asked, doubtful.

"Only part of it. I'm hoping I'll find out the rest soon that will complete the whole picture."

"I really appreciate all you're doing for me."

"It's part of the job."

"Is sleeping with the boss part of the job, too?"

"You're not my boss."

"Partner, then?"

"No, this goes under extracurricular activities." She kissed him and soon they forgot all about Jade and Martha.

Afterward they lay naked under the blankets and watched a film. Then someone knocked on the door.

"I'm not expecting anyone," Hannah said.

Amal lazily stroked her back, making no motion to move. "Call out and ask who it is."

"Probably a salesman. If I'm quiet they'll go away."

The person knocked again. "Hannah, it's me."

Hannah leaped to her feet. "Oh, damn. It's my sister!"

Chapter 12

Hannah scrambled into her clothes. "You've got to hide."

Amal gaped at her, bewildered. "Why?"

"Because she can't see you here. Especially like this."

Abigail knocked again. "Hannah? I know you're in there."

"I'll be with you in a minute," she shouted. She quickly gathered Amal's clothes and shoved them into his chest. "Go into my bedroom and stay there. Be as quiet as you can."

"But—"

"Just do it. I'll get rid of her."

Amal started to walk away.

"Take the blanket, too."

He glared at her and then took the blanket and walked into her bedroom, slamming the door.

Hannah quickly glanced around the room to make

sure that there was no evidence of him remaining and then went to the front door. "Abigail."

"What were you doing?" Abigail asked, looking around the place with suspicion. She was taller than Hannah, and her hair fell to her shoulders in tight braids, unlike Hannah's straightened style. She had the innocent, adorable face of a doe and the eyes of a fox. She was attractive, though people usually forgot that when she opened her mouth.

"I was just tidying up."

"I thought I heard a door slam."

"Probably one of the neighbors. What do you want?"

"I don't want anything. I just came to see you. Is that a crime?"

"No," Hannah said, already feeling worn of her sister's testiness. "I just—"

"You haven't come by the house recently."

"I've been busy and—"

"And you're always busy. Too busy to see us. So we have to come and see you."

Hannah took a deep breath. She wouldn't get upset. "It's nice to see you. Come and sit down."

Abigail sat on the couch, and Hannah sat in front of her. She fought back a gasp when she noticed Amal's underpants peeking out from under the couch near Abigail's foot. How could she have missed them? She jumped to her feet. "Let's go sit in the kitchen."

"Why?" Abigail said, startled by her sister's behavior. "I'm comfortable here."

"Would you like anything to eat or drink?"

"No, I'm fine."

Hannah glanced at the underwear again, wondering how she could snatch them without her sister knowing.

When she looked up she saw Amal standing in the hallway with the blanket around his waist, pointing to her. She gestured for him to return to the bedroom.

Abigail frowned at her. "What's wrong?"

Hannah pretended to swat the air. "Oh, just one of those annoying little bugs," she said when Amal leaned against the wall and didn't move. She narrowed her eyes at him. He just smiled.

"We've gotten a lot done on the house," Abigail said, settling into her seat as though she planned to stay a while. "But no one will tell us how it's being paid for."

"I've taken care of it."

"How?"

Hannah sat next to her sister so that she wouldn't have to look at Amal and could grab his underpants. "I've made arrangements. You don't have to worry about anything."

"It's all legal, right? I know a lot of Mafia people work in construction."

Hannah sighed. Her sister was ever the drama queen. "You're going to be all right." She patted her on the back while trying to move the underwear under the couch with her foot. Since she couldn't get to it, she might as well hide it. "You and Mom and Dad can stay in the house for the rest of your lives."

"Did you know we got landscaping, too? You should see it. It's beautiful. It's like a palace."

"That's great."

"No, it's not great," she snapped. "You should talk to them. We don't want things too extravagant, or they could price us out of the neighborhood."

"I'm sure they know what they're doing."

"Maybe." Abigail stood and started to turn.

Hannah grabbed her hand. "Where are you going?"

Abigail frowned. "I just need to go to the bathroom."

"Okay." She released her and watched her disappear into the bathroom. She then fell on her knees and tried to reach for Amal's underpants, which she'd kicked underneath the couch. But she'd moved the garment farther than she'd expected, so she had to get on her stomach to reach it. She snatched it with triumph and raced to her room just as Abigail was coming out of the bathroom. "What's that?" she asked.

Hannah glanced down at what was in her hands. "It's nothing. I'm just going to put them in my room."

"They look like men's briefs."

"They're mine."

"Yours?"

"Yes, it's a boy's cut. Excuse me." She went into her room and found Amal sitting on her bed.

"I told you to stay in here."

"I needed to get my—"

She threw them at him. "Now get dressed, be quiet and stay put."

Amal pulled on his underpants. "Is your sister always so miserable?"

Hannah put her finger to her mouth and then closed the door. She returned to the living room, where her sister was flipping through a book.

"You're acting kinda strange," Abigail said, putting the book down. "You know, if you don't want me here you can just say so. I just thought you'd want to know what's happening with *our* parents."

"It's not that," Hannah said, resisting rubbing her hands together, eager to see her sister leave. "I've just been stressed. I really appreciate you coming by."

"Sure you do," Abigail said, unconvinced. She walked toward the door and then stopped and pointed at a pair of male shoes. "What's that?" She turned to her. "And don't tell me they're yours."

"Abigail, I—"

"You're seeing someone, aren't you?" Her eyes widened. "You're hiding a man."

"Listen."

"Where is he?" She opened the hall closet and peeked inside. "I'm not leaving until I meet him."

"You'll meet him soon."

"Why not now?"

"Yes, why not now?" Amal said, coming into the living room. He held out his hand to Abigail. "I'm Amal Harper."

She stared at him, spellbound.

Hannah reluctantly gestured to her and made introductions. "This is my sister, Abigail."

"A pleasure to meet you."

"Wait," Abigail said. "Your name sounds familiar."

"Well, that's it. You've met." Hannah grabbed her sister's arm and tried to drag her toward the door. "Glad you stopped by. Now it's time to go."

Abigail pointed an accusatory finger at Amal. "You're the womanizer. Yes, I've read about you." She gave him a quick once-over. "You may have your handsome face and fine clothes, but I know what you really are. A heartbreaker." She turned to Hannah. "How could you dump Jacob for him? What will Mom and Dad say?"

Hannah opened the door. "Nothing, because they don't need to know."

"They'll have to know."

"And you'll delight in being the one to tell them."

Abigail sauntered past without saying a word.

Hannah closed the door. Amal rested his hands on her shoulders. "This was bound to happen."

"I wish you hadn't met her first. She'll put you at a disadvantage."

"It's okay. Let me meet your parents and then we'll go from there."

With the help of Bonnie's aunt and her connections, Hannah managed to get an appointment at the spa where Martha went for beauty treatments. But when she got the talkative Natalie Brimmer, a young nail apprentice, instead of the owner she had hoped for, Hannah feared she'd been met with another dead end. She plastered on a smile as Natalie chatted about her boyfriend, her recent trip to Disneyland and the telenovelas she loved to watch to practice her Spanish. Twice Hannah tried to get her to talk about Mrs. Walker (she didn't know much) or anything else about the owner, who was one of Martha's closest friends (she had nothing to share). So Hannah anxiously glanced at her watch, wondering what her next step should be.

"But my friend has a more exciting life than I do," Natalie said.

"Really?" Hannah said, fighting back a yawn.

"Yes, you wouldn't think so, because she's a nurse and works in this small hospital thirty minutes out of town. Her mother asked why she chose such a dinky place, but she said that she likes the people there and that it's run well."

"Hmm."

"Anyway, several months ago this rich family rented

an entire floor of the hospital so that their daughter could have a baby. I mean, they got the top suite, and it all seemed very mysterious. At first my friend thought it was some celebrity, but it wasn't. Though they seemed very wealthy, it all didn't make any sense. Why would they go to a place like that? If I had money I'd go to a top city hospital, let me tell you. Plus it was a high-risk pregnancy, with the mother having gestational diabetes and high blood pressure."

Hannah glanced up, intrigued, thinking of Martha's medications. "Really?"

Natalie nodded. "There were two times my friend said they were afraid they'd lose the mother and the baby. But with our obesity crisis, what do you expect?"

"Obesity crisis?" Hannah asked, trying to follow Natalie's logic.

"Yeah, I mean, the girl was huge. I think it's disgusting the way people are eating themselves to death. I mean, how can you have a healthy baby when you're not even healthy yourself?"

Hannah ignored the apprentice's coarse words as her mind quickly put the missing pieces together. A baby? Could the image she'd seen of Jade been the picture of a pregnant woman rather than just an overweight one? Was that what Martha was desperate to hide?

The moment she left the salon, Hannah went online to check birth records from about six to eight months ago for local hospitals in the area, trying to find proof to confirm her suspicions.

Over an hour later she sat staring at the screen in shock, now understanding why the Walkers had kept the secret. It changed everything.

Chapter 13

"So what did you want to tell me?" Amal asked as they sat in her office. "You sounded very somber on the phone."

"I have some very important news to tell you." Hannah clasped her hands together. She'd practiced all night how she'd tell him, but she still wasn't sure. Dread mixed with anticipation.

"And you couldn't tell me over dinner?"

"No."

His good humor fell. "Is it bad news?"

"I found out why Jade gained weight and then disappeared from view. Why the Walkers want to divert your attention by keeping your inventory and destroying your business."

"Why?"

Hannah laid her hands flat on the table and held his gaze. "Jade had a son and he's yours."

Amal didn't move. He didn't blink, and he didn't swallow. He just stared at her, registering no emotion.

Hannah cautiously continued. "He was born about eight months after your breakup."

Amal shook his head. "No, I can't have a son."

"But you do."

"Jade would have told me she was pregnant. She wouldn't have kept that from me."

"Amal. He's yours."

He narrowed his gaze and kept his voice soft. "Why are you lying to me?"

"I'm not."

"Then why would she? Not telling me she was pregnant is kind of a lie, isn't it?"

"Amal—"

He held up his fist and shook it. "Don't try to console me. I'm not in the mood."

Hannah leaned forward and glared at him. "I'm not the enemy here."

He turned away and pounded the arm of his chair. "I can't believe she didn't tell me. Why wouldn't she have told me? I would have taken care of her. Both of them. No, she wouldn't have done this to me."

Hannah looked at Amal, feeling helpless and wishing she knew how to comfort him. "She must have had her reasons."

"Maybe to punish me because I broke up with her."

"Or maybe she was afraid you'd take the baby from her. She was in bad shape at the time."

"I wouldn't have taken him away. We would have gotten married and—"

"Perhaps that's not what she wanted."

He stood. "No, it's because she cheated on me. The baby's not mine and—"

"You know that's not true."

"It has to be true," Amal shouted. "She wouldn't do this to me. Not when she knew how much I—" He paced. "No."

"I'm sure the Walkers wanted to refute it. He's yours. I know this is a lot to take in. What you can do is face the Walkers. You can get visitation."

"No," he said in a flat tone.

"No?"

"I want him."

Hannah paused. "You want to see him?"

"No. I want him. He's my son and I want to raise him. I won't let the Walkers take him from me. How old is he?"

"Seven months."

"Good. He's still young enough that it won't be too traumatic a change."

"Raising a child is a big responsibility. Are you sure you're ready for that? We could come up with visitation rights and—"

"No, I will not have the Walkers raise my son and slowly poison him against me, because I know that's what they will do. I know it sounds impulsive and crazy to you, but I want this. He's my son and he belongs with me." He looked at her, a little uncertain. "And you said Jade wanted it too, right?"

"I'm sure she did."

"Then I've made up my mind. Let's meet with their lawyer and get my son."

She screamed. She screamed until she thought her lungs would burst. How could this have happened? How could they have found out about him? She'd been so careful.

"Martha, you need to calm down," her husband said, handing her a glass of water.

Martha slapped it out of his hand, delighting in how it shattered on the ground and soaked the floor. "I will not calm down. They will not steal my baby. He's mine."

"You need to think this over."

"I have, and James stays with me."

"Harper has his rights."

"He screwed my daughter in more ways than one. Why does that give him any rights?" She turned to Peter. "Do something."

Peter shrugged in his typical blasé style. "There's nothing to do."

"What did our lawyer say?"

"Our hands are tied. Not only have they discovered about the boy, but they can prove the documents you presented were false. You'll have to release the inventory."

"He can have that junk."

"He wants the baby, too."

"I told you to just give him the things," Granville said. "Then he'd never have found out about anything. But you wanted to destroy him, too."

"I'll take him to court," Martha said.

"You'll lose," Peter said.

"No, I won't. We're going to go to court, and Amal won't touch James. I'll let the world know what kind of father he'd be."

The Walkers started a smear campaign. Going to the press and telling the heartbreaking story of their dead daughter and how Amal was trying to steal all they had left of her. They targeted high-brow papers to the most obscure.

"She's burying you," Hector said, looking at an online article that showed Amal dancing with three scantily clad women. "You've got to say something. You're being painted as a heartless playboy who only cares about wine and women."

"I used to, but I don't anymore."

"Then you need to say that. Public opinion matters."

"I have the law on my side."

"Judges can be swayed."

"I'm going to win this."

"Are you sure you want to?"

Amal stared at him. "What do you mean by that?"

"What do you know about being a father? You're getting your business back on track and you've got a great woman in your life. Do you think you can keep all that with a kid?"

"I don't have a choice."

"Yes, you do."

"No, I don't. I know what it's like to grow up without a father. I won't do that to my son."

But the custody case proved to be a nastier fight than Amal expected, one so stressful his mother decided not to appear in court with him. Hannah stayed by his side. The Walkers came into family court and presented the life he'd been leading during and after Jade's death, and it wasn't a pretty picture. And the judge, a conservative from Georgia who loved Southern gospel and donating to children's charities, was not pleased with the picture in front of her. She sent looks of disgust in Amal's direction as if she didn't know what the word *impartial* meant. Yet she admitted that she had to go with the fact that he was the biological father and Jade giving the boy the Harper surname had specified her wishes. A friend of Natasha's, who also practiced family law, was his legal representative.

"However," the judge continued, "I'm going to put my own clause down because I'm concerned for this child's welfare. You have six months to get your life into shape. You will not be seen out gallivanting with many women or anything of that nature. You'll agree to a high standard for this child, or you'll be in this court again and I'll give the Walkers full custody." She then addressed the Walkers. "I want you to know that keeping this man's child hidden was a despicable act, even though I understand your reason. Court's dismissed."

The caseworker came in with the baby in a stroller and Martha rushed over and picked him up. "No, you can't have him."

"The courts gave him the right," her husband said, standing close by.

"I don't care what the courts say."

"You can visit him," Amal said.

She held the baby tighter, tears springing to her eyes. "Don't do this to me."

"Ma'am, you have to let the baby go now," the caseworker said.

Martha shut her eyes, handed him the baby and then walked away.

Her husband looked at Amal. "You will tell us how he is, won't you? And give us updates every once in a while?"

Amal could only nod, not trusting himself to speak. He was holding his son. He felt both fear and joy. He tentatively looked down and saw a pair of big brown eyes staring back at him. He marveled at his tiny nose and mouth and fell instantly in love. Jade had named him James Romare Harper, his middle name referring to Jade's favorite African American artist, Romare Bearden. Amal's throat tightened and he fought back tears. He and Jade had created something beautiful.

Hannah touched his shoulder. "Come on. Let's go home."

"What's the matter?" Hannah asked him on their ride home. "You haven't said a word. You should be celebrating. You won. He's yours. Instead, you look worried."

"I'm just thinking about what the lawyers and judge said about me in the courtroom."

"The lawyer had to. He wanted to win."

"And the judge?"

"Has her own opinions."

"But she's right. I didn't get my son based on my character but rather on the fact that I'm his biological father and the assumption that Jade wanted me to raise him. And if I mess up, I know that the Walkers will immediately swoop in and try to take him from me."

She patted his leg and glanced at James, renamed J.R., in the rearview mirror. "You're being too hard on yourself."

He shook his head. "No, I haven't been hard enough. My reputation was well earned, and I didn't care what anybody thought or said. I was careless and sometimes tactless, but that has to change. I can't give them a reason to take my son away. I can't fail him like I did his mother."

"You won't."

"I want you to help me."

"Me? How?"

"I want to change. When you see me going off track, I want you to put me in line. I want to be a good father."

"It's not like there's a manual to being a parent. Most of it is instinctual."

"My father left when I was young. Yours is still around. You'll know more about this than I do. Please, if not for me then for J.R."

"Okay." Hannah took his hand. "I'll do it for you both."

Doreen's face beamed when Amal entered with the baby.

"Is he really ours?" she said as Amal handed him to her.

"Yes."

She gazed down at the baby. "Oh, he's beautiful. My beautiful J.R."

"Well, I'll leave you two," Hannah said, turning to the door.

"But you can't leave," Amal said, blocking her.

"This is a special time for you and your mother."

"Remember you said you wanted to have dinner with her. Well, now's a good time."

"No, it's not. It's a very important family moment."

"You can't leave me now," he said with a hint of anxiety. She'd heard it before when they'd gone shopping for baby items in preparation for J.R.'s arrival. Amal analyzed and weighed the pros and cons of each item, from diaper pails to bedding to the crib itself.

"It's going to be fine," Hannah said as Amal circled the crib and thoroughly checked every screw and groove.

"I've heard that some of these cribs can kill."

"This one won't. It's a trusted brand."

Amal shook the railing. "He deserves the best."

Hannah looped her arm through his and gave him a quick, reassuring squeeze. "And you'll give it to him," she said, making him smile.

Hannah remembered that time as she looked at him now, knowing he had to be strong and face his fears.

"You'll be fine," she said. "You have everything you need."

"What if he starts crying?"

"Your mother will help you."

"Why not you?"

"I don't know anything about babies."

He grabbed her arms. "Please don't leave me yet."

"Amal, you're his father." She wiggled out of his grasp. "You'll be fine. If he cries, he's either hungry or wet. It's not that complicated." She opened the door.

"You said I should celebrate. Why won't you help me celebrate? I'll call in whatever you want. Please."

She kissed him on the cheek. "No, you can do this. I'll call you tomorrow."

It was hard to leave him. Every step she took away from his door, she fought not to turn back, but she knew this was for the best. Amal had to believe in himself. He had to realize that he could do this. He could be a good father. Being frightened was okay.

Hannah didn't sleep that night, thinking about him and J.R. Was he really okay? Did J.R. sleep through the night? Would Amal know what to do? Would Doreen remember?

Hannah sat up in bed and slapped herself. She was worrying for no reason. This was just what they needed. Doreen would now have a purpose. She wouldn't need to do outrageous things to get attention, and now Amal had something to always remind him of Jade.

Jade. Hannah couldn't seem to escape her memory. She was the only reason Hannah was even in his life. He'd loved her. He only wanted Hannah as a convenient companion and to train him to be a father. He had a new focus now, and maybe she needed a new focus, too. She'd fallen for him too fast and too easily. She needed to gain some perspective. She doubted he thought of her the way she did him. She knew he didn't really need her to show him how to change his ways. Over the past several months they'd been together, he had changed on his own. He hadn't been to any wild parties or gone out with women. He'd devoted his time to going grocery shopping, sitting on the couch and watching sitcoms. He'd been amazingly ordinary.

He doesn't need me anymore, Hannah realized. That's why she couldn't sleep. His son had taken her place, and he deserved to. And she needed to find the strength to tell Amal goodbye.

"She hasn't called," Amal said the next morning. "Why hasn't she called?"

"Amal," Doreen said, exasperated. "You have to stop pacing like that. You're making J.R. nervous."

He glanced down at his son, who lay on the couch,

happily trying to chew on his fist. Last night had been easier and harder than he'd expected. He'd fed J.R. and changed his diaper. He had woken up twice during the night to his cries before rocking him back to sleep. He'd bathed him and fed him this morning, at each moment thinking he wanted Hannah with him. He'd wanted her by his side when he'd returned to bed, wanted to know if she'd have known of any lullabies to calm J.R. off to sleep. Yes, he did want to be a father, but to his surprise he didn't want to do it without her. But he knew he was being unfair. It wasn't something she was ready for. He could see it on her face as she left him yesterday. This was the life he'd chosen, not her. He knew his true fear wasn't about one missed phone call but that he might never hear from her again.

"Why don't you call her?" Doreen asked.

Because he knew the signs when someone was pulling away. He'd done it many times. He knew how to dump someone. He'd just never had it happen to him. But she said she was going to help him, and she wouldn't lie about that. Would she?

"Let's take J.R. out for a stroll," Doreen said, picking the baby up.

His mother already looked radiant. She fell into the role of grandmother easily. He was glad to see her happy. He remembered how annoyed she'd been when he'd offered to interview nannies.

"A nanny? You don't need one. You have me."

"But, Mom, you have your own life."

"No, now my life is his. I'll take care of him."

"You'll need assistance."

"Don't you trust me?"

Not completely yet. "It will just be for a couple of months."

She finally relented. He had a nanny service scheduled to come next week and hoped Hannah would be there to help him select. She would be. He wouldn't let her walk out on him, even if she wanted to.

Chapter 14

"Tell me about this man you're seeing," Hannah's mother said as they ate dinner. She'd been invited to dinner and knew better than to refuse, especially since she didn't have a work-related excuse to give them. She still felt guilty for not calling Amal as she'd promised, but she couldn't talk to him yet.

Hannah shot a glance at her sister, who feigned an innocent expression. "The house looks great."

"Don't change the subject," her mother said. She was an imposing woman who'd given Abigail her striking height and Hannah her bold gaze. "Tell us about this man."

"I'm not really seeing anyone." *Anymore.*

"Your sister told us you're seeing a man. That he's not a man of good character."

"That's not true."

"Then why haven't you told us anything about him yet? When did you expect to introduce us?"

Not anytime soon. "Mom, I—"

"What's his name?"

"Amal Harper," Abigail said.

"Harper? Why does his name sound familiar?"

"Because she helped him win a case. She's his lawyer."

"I wasn't his lawyer," Hannah corrected.

"Where was he born?"

"Rhode Island."

"He's black American?"

Hannah sighed. "Yes."

"Is that why you didn't want to introduce us?"

"No."

"He has a reputation," Abigail said with a superior
grin. "With the ladies."

"Is that right?" her father asked.

"He's a good man," Hannah said.

"Is that what he's gotten you to believe?" Abigail
said, doubtful. "Mom, you should have read the papers
and seen the pictures of him—"

"He has a very successful business," Hannah cut in
defensively. "And a great relationship with his family.
Especially his mother."

"He's good to her?" her mother asked with interest.

"Yes."

"And he has a child," Abigail added in a singsongy
voice.

"Will you shut up!"

Her mother slapped Hannah's arm. "Don't talk to
your sister like that."

"Why not?" Hannah asked, rubbing her arm. "She's
just stirring up trouble."

"Is he a married man?"

"Of course not."

"How old is the child?"

"Several months."

"And where is the mother?"

"Deceased."

"He didn't even know he had a child," Abigail said.

Hannah shook her head. "It's not that simple."

Her mother nodded. "Oh, I now see. This man wants you to look after his child."

"That's not—"

"That's the way I see it," her mother cut in. "Why would he suddenly change his ways for you?" She shook her head. "I can't believe you'd leave nice and wonderful Jacob to be snatched up by another woman so you can fool around with someone like this. You're just trying to hurt me."

"It's not like that."

"I don't like this Harper fellow. Break up with him immediately."

"Mom, you haven't even met him."

"And I don't plan to."

"You're judging someone you don't understand."

"Tell me what I don't understand about a man who doesn't know about his own child? Who goes through women, but only decides to settle down when he needs someone to look after his offspring. He's not good for you. You will have to put your career aside for his needs, and you didn't work hard so that you can be a nurse-maid to someone else's baby."

"Fine," Hannah said, pushing jollof rice around on her plate. She wasn't going to introduce them anyway, and her mother was right. She had her career to think about.

"I want to meet him," her dad said. He was a big, good-looking man of few words.

Her head shot up and she stared at him. "I'm not planning to marry him."

He shook his gray head. "I don't care. I still want to meet him. Unless you're ashamed of us."

Hannah hung her head. "It's not that. We've broken up."

"He broke up with you?"

"No, I broke up with him. Mom's right. I'm not ready for that kind of pressure in my life."

"So he *is* trying to turn you into a nursemaid?"

"Dad, they don't use terms like that. The word is *nanny.*"

"He wants to make you that?"

"No, but—"

"You just said he's a good man with a fine business who takes care of his family. Why did you break up with him?"

"Because he's no good," his wife said.

"No," her father said, his gaze never leaving Hannah's face. "Because she's scared. He means a lot to her." He slammed his hand on the table. "It's settled. He'll come for dinner this Friday." He held up his hand. "And that's final."

Hannah bit her lip, knowing that it was.

But she didn't tell Amal about her parents' invitation. She went to work instead and hoped that his schedule would fill up so fast that by the time she called him he'd have to refuse. She had begun to get new clients, small cases, but she would focus on work and forget all about him. She rested her legs on her desk and smiled.

Her smile fell when the door swung open and Amal walked in holding a car seat with J.R. cozily inside. "Why didn't you call me?"

She let her feet crash to the ground. "What?"

"You promised you'd call me. Did you forget?"

Hannah closed the door, even though Bonnie was the only person in the reception area. She didn't want her to hear. "You don't have to shout."

"Why?"

"I just thought you needed time to get your new life in order."

"You're part of my life."

"Is that a new look for you? The business suit and the carrier?"

"Mom's getting her nails done, so I'm looking after him."

"You look great. Is he sleeping through the night?"

"You haven't answered my question."

"Yes, I did."

"Truthfully. It's been a week."

"Has it?" Hannah said with feigned surprise. "Wow, how time flies."

"You said you'd help me—"

"You don't need me to help you. You'll be a great father. I realized we're going in different directions and you need to focus on your family and I need to focus on my work and—"

"That's complete B.S."

Bonnie knocked on the door and then poked her head inside before Hannah could reply. "Your mother's on the phone," Bonnie said, ignoring Hannah's exaggerated gestures behind Amal's back to be quiet. "She wants to know if Amal is allergic to anything."

Hannah glared at her, knowing her friend was setting her up because she knew about her father's request.

Bonnie just smiled. "What should I tell her?"

Hannah bared her teeth and then changed her expression when Amal turned to her.

"What is she talking about?" he asked.

"The dinner at her parents' house this Friday," Bonnie said casually. "They're expecting to meet you."

He spun to her. "Expecting me?"

"Yes."

He turned to Hannah again. "When were you going to tell me?"

"I was waiting for the right moment."

He looked at Bonnie. "Tell her mother that I'm not allergic to anything and I'm looking forward to meeting her."

"Okay," Bonnie said and then left.

"You don't know what you're walking into," Hannah said. "My mother can be difficult, you've met my sister and my father is—"

"Family is family. I don't care. Were you going to tell me?"

"You have a lot already going on in your life. Trust me, you don't need this."

"I'll tell you what I need. I need to know that I can depend on you. That I can trust you. I knew I could before and I need to know that I can now."

Hannah sat on her desk and sighed, feeling as if she were under an anvil tied to a slowly unraveling rope. He didn't understand, but maybe meeting her family would help him to know what she couldn't tell him. At that moment, she looked over and saw him with his son, and for one brief second she'd wished he was theirs. That they were a family and that he'd want to marry her and would love her as he had Jade. She didn't want him to learn the truth—that a man who didn't want to marry had stolen the heart of a woman who did.

She took his hand, although inside she was trembling. "I'm sorry. I won't bail on you again."

"Is that a promise?"

"Yes," she said.

He bent down and kissed her and then cupped her face. "I missed you."

His tenderness made her love him more, and she hated herself for it. She bit her lip and lowered her gaze so he wouldn't see her tears.

"What's wrong?"

Hannah blinked back her tears. "I'm sorry I let you down. I just—"

"It's okay." Amal lifted her chin and grinned, reminding her of the first day she'd seen him. "You can make it up to me."

"How?"

"I'm interviewing nannies today."

"Okay."

"And I want you to help me."

"What time are they coming?"

"Starting at six."

"I'll be there." She sighed and then decided to take the plunge. "Can I hold him?"

"Sure."

Hannah bent over to take J.R. out of the carrier, which Amal had placed on a table in her office. She made a face and he smiled. "He's amazingly good-natured."

"Yes, he doesn't cry much."

Hannah tickled the baby's stomach. "So you don't have your daddy's nasty temper. You lucky boy." She looked up at Amal and smiled. "And now we need to find you the right nanny."

At first Hannah thought selecting a nanny would be an easy prospect until she looked at the line of women waiting in the hallway and shook her head—they were all younger than thirty, and very attractive of all shades. Hannah turned to Amal and said, "What agency did you go to get these women? The Ford Modeling Agency?"

"What do you mean?"

"Have you seen these women?"

He looked out in the hall and beamed. "This is amazing."

"Where are they from?"

"Hector made the call."

"They all look like models."

He straightened his shirt. "I know."

"If you want to change your image, you cannot choose a woman who looks like that." She gestured to a woman in a low-cut blouse and tight miniskirt.

"Why not? There's no reason for you to be jealous."

"This is not about me being jealous," Hannah said in a tight voice, making a note to talk to Hector when she got a chance. "This goes back to your image. Everyone will assume you've hired her for more than one thing. And second, I don't think any of these women came here for the baby."

"So we're not going to interview any of them?" Amal said, disappointed.

"No."

"Not even one or two just for the fun of it?"

"No."

He put his hands together and made a pitiful face. "Please."

Hannah reluctantly smiled and relented. "All right. No more than four."

The first one was a definite "no." She barely glanced at Hannah and took no interest in J.R. She just stared at Amal as though mesmerized. The second prospect was just as mesmerized but a bit more cunning. She made J.R. smile and shook Hannah's hand, but her grip was too strong and her smile forced. The third was very young and anxious to please. The last was the hardest one for Hannah. The woman was gorgeous, intelligent and funny, and to Hannah's surprise she liked her. She knew Amal liked her, too. Her name was Camille Jackson, and she wasn't too flashy and would be good for his image. She had a confidence and a sense of responsibility, as though she was someone they could trust.

"You could do so many things," Hannah said. "Why be a nanny?"

"Because I enjoy it. I have great references."

"Yes, I see that. We'll get back to you."

Camille left.

"She was the best, don't you think?" Amal said.

"Yes," Hannah admitted with some hesitation.

Amal turned to his mother, who'd sat in the corner of the room the entire time with her arms folded. "Mom, what do you think?"

"I still don't see why you need a nanny when you have me."

"Because I can't take him every time you want to visit your friend or get your hair done."

"I don't do it all the time," she mumbled.

"It's just for a while."

"I think you should hire Camille," Hannah said.

Amal turned to her, hopeful. "Really?"

"Yes, she's perfect for you."

"You mean *us*."

"Right. You and J.R.," she corrected.

"No," he said, frowning. "I mean you and me. I want you to feel good about this, too. I won't hire her if you're not comfortable."

"I'm fine. She's great."

"I'll call her right away and also talk to the agency head." He left the room.

"Have you lost your mind?" Doreen asked. "Do you really want a woman like that around Amal?"

"I really liked her."

"Don't sabotage this. I know what you're doing." Doreen crossed the room and stood in front of her. "I know my son. He may get his head turned, but you're the one for him. The right one. I knew it the first moment I met you, and you're the right one for J.R., too. I have never seen Amal so settled since he met you. You bring a sense of stability into our lives. But I know we're good for you, too. You've got a good thing here. Don't throw it away."

Amal approached them. "She says she can start tomorrow. Now let me take you two beautiful ladies out for dinner."

They enjoyed a simple dinner at a local diner that had enough space for a high chair for J.R. Doreen delighted in the unfamiliar atmosphere and the sight of fried clams, French fries and soda. Doreen shared stories about her younger days and the trouble she used to get into, with Amal sharing some of his own. They laughed and teased, enjoying each other's company.

"Stay the night," Amal said after they returned home and put J.R. to bed.

Hannah tugged on his shirt with a coy grin. "I can't be your sex toy anymore, Daddy."

Amal wrapped his arms around her waist and then let one hand slide down her backside. "Daddies can still have fun."

She moved his wandering hand back to her waist. "Not when he has to wake up in the middle of the night."

Amal pressed her close to him, his tone deepening. "He sleeps through sometimes. Come on."

Amal convinced her to stay in more ways than one. The baby woke up at three, and they both got up to help him go back to sleep.

"I'm so glad you stayed," he said when they returned to his bedroom.

Hannah slipped into bed. "Me, too."

"I lied."

"About what?"

"This. It hasn't been easy. I once wore two different shoes to work, I forgot to shave and I nearly boiled his formula and had him spit up on my shirt and didn't know it until someone pointed it out."

Hannah laughed. "Welcome to parenthood."

"But I love him."

"I know."

"I didn't think it would happen so fast, and for a second I wondered if my father ever thought about me that way."

"I'm sure he did."

"I'm not. But that's okay because I'm not going to be like him. No matter what, I'll stick around."

Amal lay in bed with Hannah by his side, feeling as if he could fly. His life was coming together at last. He had someone to look after J.R., his mother was happy and Hannah was back by his side. Now he just had to meet her parents.

Chapter 15

"A pleasure to meet you, sir," Amal said when Mr. Olaniyi answered the door.

"You don't even have the decency to bow to your elders?" Abigail sneered behind her father.

Hannah hit her. "He's American. He doesn't know those customs."

"You could have taught him."

Amal looked at Hannah, unsure. "Did I do something wrong?"

"No," her father said, shaking his hand. "Please come in."

When the two men turned, Hannah pinched her sister hard.

"Ow!" Abigail cried, making a face.

"That was a warning," Hannah said. "Try to be nice, or I'll leave a mark next time."

They settled at the table and her mother came out

with some of the food. "You're looking lovely, Mrs. Olaniyi," Amal said.

Hannah inwardly cringed. Her mother was wearing a simple "market woman" outfit. Its colorful design could easily be mistaken for something grander by someone not familiar with their custom of dress. But in truth her outfit was as insulting as a woman wearing a sweat suit to a fancy dinner.

Mrs. Olaniyi just shot him a look before returning to the kitchen.

Hannah leaned over and whispered to Amal, "Remember to touch with your right hand."

He nodded, but twice he nearly forgot when he reached for a shared dish, and Hannah had to kick him to remember. In their culture, the left hand was reserved for personal hygiene. The conversation was stilted. Although Amal tried to charm her mother, she answered with short responses. Abigail took delight in the tension. Fortunately, Hannah's father picked up most of the slack and helped to keep the conversation flowing. Soon he and Amal were talking about soccer games, economics and world events as if they were old friends.

"At least Dad likes him," Abigail said in the kitchen after they'd cleared the plates and left Amal and their father talking in the living room.

"He's still no Jacob," her mother inserted.

"No."

"And these black Americans don't marry their women. They give them children mostly and sometimes will live off them, but they don't marry them."

"Black Americans do marry."

"Not many," she scoffed.

"Amal doesn't need to live off of any woman," Hannah said. "He's established."

"And what are his thoughts on marriage?" her mother asked.

"He'd rather tie himself to a tugboat and be dragged across the Atlantic before he ties himself to any woman," Abigail said.

Her mother's eyes widened. "He said that?"

"No," Hannah said.

"Yes, he did," Abigail said. "He said it in an article. That was a direct quote."

"I'm sure it was a long time ago."

"Not that long," Abigail countered.

"And you want to be with a man like that?" her mother asked, stunned.

Hannah shook her head. "We're not even close to even beginning to talk about marriage."

"And you likely won't," she said with certainty. "Just you wait and see. A year will pass and he'll ask you to move in, and that will be the extent of his commitment to you."

Hannah knew she couldn't reply, because her mother was right. Amal wasn't the marrying kind.

In the living room Amal sat with Mr. Olaniyi, feeling a little more at home. He'd never had an older man as a mentor and hoped he could soon count him as one. Her father had wisdom, and Amal appreciated that, in spite of his disability, he had a nice outlook on life. Amal had so many questions he wanted to share with another man. Like the times when he watched Hannah with his son and mother and saw her competence and wondered if he fit in. Women always seemed to automatically be seen as the nurturers and caretakers. Most of his life he was surrounded by women. Could he be just as important?

"So, you have a son," Mr. Olaniyi said.

"Yes, right now he's with his nanny." Amal cleared his throat and tried to make his voice light, as if his next statement didn't matter. "Sometimes when I see him with Hannah, she's so capable and strong. I don't think Hannah needs me."

Mr. Olaniyi nodded soberly, taking Amal's statement with the weight it deserved, sensing his fear. "I know how you feel. After my accident I felt so useless to my wife and daughters. I couldn't be the husband and father I wanted to be. But after I got over pitying myself, I realized that that fact didn't mean I wasn't a husband and a father. What I could do may have changed, but not my role. So I've done my best to continue to nurture and maintain those relationships.

"It's not easy, but important. I learned to listen to their needs—it's amazing how tranquil some women are. They just want you to listen. Not go out and fix their problems for them, just to listen and know they've been heard. That's it. It's a secret I pass on to you. Sometimes you'll just be a shoulder to cry on, and that will be enough." He showed him a picture of Hannah in fourth grade playing a game of tennis.

"You know, she gave me a note one day that I'll never forget. It wasn't sentimental or flowery—just a few simple words. 'Thanks for being there.' Not thanks for giving me the best advice, thanks for being rich or strong, just thanks for being present in her life. Through the good grades and the bad, the brilliant sport games and the failures, being that steady person she could depend on is all that mattered. It's easier to run away. That's why a lot of men do it."

At the end of the evening Mrs. Olaniyi gave them a plate of food wrapped in aluminum foil to take with them. Hannah grabbed Amal's arm and led him to the car, relieved the night was over.

"Your mother doesn't like me," Amal said.

Hannah squeezed his arm in reassurance. "She'll get used to you."

"Your sister doesn't like me, either."

Hannah laughed and then kissed him on the cheek. "Don't worry. She doesn't like anyone, including me."

As Hannah hurried to her apartment, the summer heat threatened to melt her into the sidewalk. She thought about the dinner she and Amal had with her parents over two months ago. Amal was still trying to think of ways to persuade her mother to like him, but Hannah knew there was only one way he could— although she'd never mention it to him. She remembered how she tried to sidestep the issue a few days ago.

"So what did she like about Jacob?" Amal had asked as they pushed J.R. through the park. She'd gotten used to the leisurely weekend strolls with just the three of them. Camille, their nanny, had offered to come, but Amal always gave her the time off. Hannah felt almost like a family when they stopped to look at the geese and point out different sights to J.R. But their conversations always veered toward her mother.

She playfully swatted him on the butt. "I told you to stop worrying."

"How can I? It's a problem."

"I'm still with you, aren't I? Not all women are subject to falling for your many charms." She stopped and bent down to smile at J.R. "Isn't it a great day?"

"He can hardly talk yet. Why do you keep asking him questions?"

"Because he understands me." She tickled J.R.'s stomach, making him giggle. "Your daddy doesn't know how smart you are. Do you know how much I love you?" She extended her arms out to the side and J.R. imitated her. It had become a game between them. "I love you more than this much," she said and then hugged him, and he giggled even more. She looked up at Amal in triumph. "See? He understands."

Amal shook his head. "He's just mimicking you."

Hannah looked at J.R. "Your daddy has a lot to learn."

Amal took her hand and lifted her to her feet. "That's why I have you to teach me," he said and then pressed his lips on hers. She never knew a man could taste better each time.

Hannah was thinking about Amal's words and kiss as she walked to her apartment, but she stopped when a man stepped in her path. She glanced to her side and noticed the limo.

She rested her hands on her hips. "How come this feels so familiar?"

Peter gestured to the limo with his head. "You know what to do."

"You haven't said 'please' yet."

He sighed with exaggerated annoyance. "Please."

"That's better."

Peter bent down, turned his cheek to her and tapped it. Hannah stared at him for a moment and then laughed, remembering what she'd done before. She playfully patted his cheek and then stepped inside the limo. To her surprise Martha wasn't sitting there, but her husband, Granville. He held out his hand. "I never got a chance to formerly introduce myself before in the courtroom. I'm Granville Thompson."

"And I'm—"

"Yes," he interrupted. "I know who you are. That's why I need to talk to you. You're the only one who can help me."

"Help?" Hannah said just to make sure she'd heard correctly.

"Yes." He sighed. "Martha is not doing well. She hasn't been well since we lost the boy. It's just been too much for her. Right after the custody hearing she went to bed and hasn't left it since. I think she's dying, or at least willing herself to."

"I'm sorry," Hannah said, genuinely concerned. "But what can I do?"

"She's too proud to speak to Amal, and I'm sure he wouldn't allow it anyway—"

"Allow what?" Hannah asked, eager for him to get to the point.

"She needs to see the boy. Just for one day. Come by with the child and let her see him. I'm sure that's all she needs."

Hannah bit her lip. "I don't know."

"Just once," he pleaded. "I'll make it worth your while."

"I don't need your money. This is risky. There's not just Amal, but J.R.'s nanny and his grandmother."

"I'm sure you'll find a way around it just to give Martha one glimpse of him. Her heart is broken. I won't say that what we did was right, but she's already been punished. I'm asking you to do this for her, please."

It was a lot to ask. Hannah knew that Amal wouldn't say yes. He was still very bitter against them, but she felt Martha did have a right to see her grandson. From the worry on Granville's face, he felt desperate, and she knew that feeling. She'd been there when her parents were about to lose their house. "All right. Just one time. And I'll be there the entire time. I won't let J.R. leave my sight."

"Understood. Come this Thursday. I'll pick you up at—"

"No, you don't need to pick me up. I'll come to your house with J.R. in the late afternoon."

"Okay, we'll be ready. Thank you for doing this."

"Thank me later. I haven't done anything yet. I have to see if I can make this work first."

But when the day arrived, Hannah wasn't sure she could pull it off. She told Doreen and Camille she wanted to take J.R. to a "Mother and Baby" workshop to give them both a break.

"That sounds like a great idea," Doreen said.

Camille frowned, uncertain. "Why don't I come with you?" she said.

"Because I'd like to bond with him on my own," Hannah replied.

Camille folded her arms in challenge. "But I'm hired to look after him."

"Yes, but this is important to Hannah," Doreen said. "She's like his mother."

"But she isn't his mother. Not yet at least. You haven't shown interest like this before. Why now?"

Hannah just looked at Camille, seeing how in the

months she'd worked there she'd taken a higher position than what she'd been hired to do. Now she was blurring the lines between her place with the baby and with Amal. "I've always shown interest in J.R. and—"

"Not like this. You didn't even want me to come with J.R. when you took Amal to meet your parents. Why is that? You didn't want them to know he had a son?"

"Why are you speaking to her like that?" Doreen asked, dismayed. "She's the one who got you hired."

"No," Camille said with a cool smile. "I was hired because of Amal—"

"Mr. Harper," Hannah corrected.

"He lets me call him Amal."

Yes, regretfully he did. She'd tried to convince Amal to be more formal with the nanny, but that had failed.

"She should call you Mr. Harper," Hannah had told him one evening as they cleared up the dinner dishes.

Amal had shuddered. "It sounds strange to me."

"But it makes you too familiar." She'd placed dishes in the sink.

"Leave the dishes."

"I need to get them washed."

He'd turned her to him and searched her face. "No, you don't." He'd rested his hands on her shoulders. "Tell me why you're upset."

"I don't like how she addresses you."

"She's in my home and I trust her. It's no big deal." He'd slid his hands down her sides and then settled on her waist. "There's no reason to be jealous."

Hannah had removed his hands and turned. "I'm not jealous." But that had been a lie. Part of her was jealous that this beautiful young woman had the same access to Amal that she had, except in the bedroom. Hannah sensed that if Camille had her way, she would have access in there, too. Camille was more dangerous than she'd realized. Doreen was right—Hannah had sabotaged a good thing, but she would fix it. She'd turned the faucet on full blast, wishing she knew how.

Amal had reached past her and turned it off and then wrapped his arms around her waist and held her snugly. "Look, it's an ego thing. I like pretty women calling me by my first name, but it doesn't mean anything more than that."

Hannah had dipped her hand in the water and then flicked it in his face. "Your ego needs an adjustment."

Amal had wiped his face and laughed. "It's nothing."

"To you maybe, but what about her?"

His gaze had dipped to Hannah's mouth. "What about her?"

"You may be giving her the wrong impression."

He'd unbuttoned the top of her blouse. "Huh?"

She'd covered his hand. "Amal, pay attention."

"You just gave me an idea. Let's go take a quick shower."

She'd grabbed his face. "Focus. We're talking about Camille."

"But I don't want to."

"This is important. I think—"

He'd swung her into his arms. "Stop thinking."

"But Camille—"

He'd headed out of the kitchen. "Forget about her," he'd said, and soon gave her plenty of reasons to.

But Hannah remembered it now as she looked at Camille and realized what her fear had been. "That doesn't mean you two are close."

"Amal makes the rules, not you…and I work for *him*.

I'm here to do what he pays me to do—look after his son, and that's exactly what I'm going to do. We all have roles. You're Amal's girlfriend. I'm J.R.'s nanny. You fulfill your role and I'll fulfill mine."

"Fine." Hannah took out her cell phone and started to dial.

"What are you doing?"

"I'm calling Amal to let him know that you're refusing to let me take J.R. with me."

Camille snatched the phone away. "I didn't say that."

Hannah raised her eyebrows with feigned innocence. "Didn't you? Remind me again about our roles."

Camille pursed her lips.

"Score one for Hannah." Doreen grinned. "I'm glad you realize your role. Only one of you is easily replaced."

Hannah held out her hand for her phone. Camille slapped it into her palm. "I'll be back before Amal comes home. You can take the day off."

"If anything happens to him…"

"Don't threaten me," Hannah warned. Then she took J.R. and his things and drove to the Walkers' house, fully aware she'd escaped one fire and jumped into a cauldron.

Chapter 16

The Walker mansion looked like a page out of *Architectural Digest.* The entrance featured a massive oak staircase lined with gold-framed artwork and large family portraits. Expensive Italian marble tile lined the hallway leading to a series of heavily decorated rooms with nine-foot ceilings. From what she could see, money was certainly not a problem.

Peter met her in the foyer and gave a low whistle. He seemed impressed when he saw J.R. in her arms.

"You're braver than I thought."

"You know better than to underestimate me," she said.

"I'm learning."

Granville came up to her. "I'm so glad you're here. Let me see him and take him to her."

"No, that wasn't our agreement. I'll take him to see her and I'll stay the entire time."

He relented. "Okay, follow me."

Hannah walked up the spiral staircase and then entered a grand room, where she saw a large poster bed and a small figure inside. The woman appeared minimized by the expansive room around her. Martha looked as if she'd aged years. Her eyes widened when she saw Hannah. "What are you doing here?"

"I thought you might want to see J.R."

"No." She frantically covered her eyes. "I don't want to see him."

"Are you sure?" Hannah walked over to the bed. "Just briefly." She sat on the bed. "J.R., this is Grandma."

He looked at Martha with brief interest as he would any stranger, and then his interest went to the drapery above them.

Martha lowered her hand and then reached out and touched the springy black curls on his head. He looked at her and smiled.

Her face crumbled into tears.

"Do you want us to leave?" Hannah asked.

"No, please don't. Oh, I'm so happy to see you." She hugged him. He briefly allowed her to embrace him and then tried to wiggle out of her grasp. Hannah gave him his favorite plush ball to keep him occupied. "He likes to play with this."

"Does Amal know you're here?"

"No."

"Why did you come?"

"Your husband asked me to."

"You didn't have to say yes."

"No," Hannah said. "So don't squander this moment."

"How could you do this for me when I've done such horrible things?"

"I'm hoping that one day you and Amal will reconcile for J.R.'s sake."

"He's such a wonder," she said, staring at her grandson. "At first Jade didn't know she was pregnant. After Amal left her she tried to get clean and went cold turkey, but the chills and the nausea were too much for her to take, so she reverted back, thinking that would stop it. When it didn't and she missed two cycles, that's when she knew it was something more. I was with her when she took the test. I prayed that it would come out negative because I knew what a positive response would mean. Amal would have rights I didn't want him to have."

"What do you mean?"

"Jade was in a terrible state at the time, still in the grips of her addiction. Disappearing at night and meeting with awful people. I knew that if Amal found out he would take the baby from us. When we found out the results, Jade wanted to tell him, but I persuaded her not to, that he'd only want the baby and not her. I was only trying to protect my daughter. I didn't realize how much I'd hurt her instead. She went into a program that helped her deal with her addiction, but then she ate instead. She stopped talking to me. I wanted to take her abroad, but she refused. She wanted to be close to Amal even if he didn't want her. She'd sometimes follow him without him knowing."

"Why didn't you do something then? Why didn't you tell him?"

"Because then he would have seen what a mess she was. She only cared about him. She made him her world. She always had. She didn't start a business because it meant something to her. She did it all for him. She didn't care about the baby she was carrying. She just had it because she wanted a part of him with her. If I hadn't stopped her she would have begged him to take her back."

"But instead you told her that he wouldn't want her," Hannah guessed. "Especially nearly seventy pounds overweight, not counting the baby's weight. Yes, I saw the pictures. I saw what she'd become."

"He did that to her!" Martha said with such fury that it startled J.R.

Hannah caressed the baby's cheek and rubbed his back. "It's okay, Grandma's not angry." But Hannah could see that she was and was trying hard to hold it under control.

"She developed high blood pressure and diabetes," Martha said in a low whisper. "We'd finally gotten her off one set of pills only to put her on others. I told everyone that she just had weight issues. I didn't want them to know the truth. And I kept the secret well hidden. When she was close to her due date, I kept her at home. But I'll admit that it got to the point when I couldn't stand to see her eat. It disgusted me."

"She was in pain."

"She did it to hurt me. She knew how much being healthy meant to me, how important it was for a young woman to keep their figure and face. She used to be so beautiful."

"She was still beautiful."

"Don't give me that inner-beauty nonsense. She was being childish because she wasn't getting her way. You know, she was eating her way through her third spicy burrito when she went into labor," Martha said with a cruel laugh. "She was nearly sick and it served her right for trying to spite me in that way. We took her to a small hospital out of town and put her under another name. She was in labor for ten hours, begging me to call Amal, pleading with me, but I didn't listen. I told her that she didn't need him because I was there. She finally focused on her breathing and gave birth to James. But the stress of labor was too much for her heart, and a week later she suffered a massive heart attack and died. All because of him."

Hannah could hear the bitterness in Martha's voice every time she said Amal's name. "But the papers listed her death as a suicide as a result of an overdose." Jade dying from a heart attack had not been mentioned during the custody trial.

Martha looked up at her. "Money can buy many things. Even a coroner's report."

"You told her lies. You kept her away from the man she loved, a man who loved her."

"He wouldn't have abandoned her if—"

"He left her because he couldn't help her and neither could you, and that's why you hate him. You wanted him to work the miracle even you couldn't. And now you hate Amal because of your guilt and your regrets. You've tormented yourself with the thought that Jade might still be here if you'd given her what she wanted."

"Yes! I know that I failed Jade. I failed her in so many ways, and I wasn't kind to her in the end because I couldn't stand to see what she'd become and I hated myself for it. When she wanted me to hug her, all I saw were her fleshy arms and round face, and that wasn't my daughter."

"She was still your daughter, Martha."

"I needed James as my second chance to make up for what I'd done. But now I don't have that." Martha rested her head back. "I don't know what to do anymore. My hatred for Amal kept me going, it kept me alive. I enjoyed blaming him for everything—he took away my Jade and now James. I hated him so much I wanted to destroy him, but it came back and destroyed me. If I'd just given him the inventory he'd never have found out about James. But you've forced me to face what I never wanted to, and now I can't hate him anymore. What am I supposed to do without something to hate?"

"Learn to love instead."

"Do you think you could bring J.R. by to see me again?"

Hannah shook her head. "Amal…"

"Just once more."

"Okay," Hannah conceded.

But "once more" turned into the next three months. Once a week Hannah came up with the excuse of the "Baby and Mother" workshop and instead took J.R. to the Walkers, where Martha played with him in the nursery and out in the garden. Her color and energy had returned. But one day as Hannah left the home under a bright autumn sky, she realized she couldn't keep the charade up forever.

Camille watched Hannah's car leave the Walkers' gate and grinned with satisfaction. She'd been following Hannah for several weeks, and now she knew it was time to use the information to her advantage. She'd thought of telling Amal about Hannah's deception right away, but she knew the longer it lasted the better it would be for her. At times it grated on her nerves how much Amal was devoted to her. It was "Hannah this" and "Hannah that." There would be no wedding bells in sight for Hannah—but perhaps, rather, for her. There was always hope. Her mother had taught her that a man's gratitude could get her anything, and she wanted to prove to Amal that she was more indispensable than Hannah was. She knew that Hannah had helped her get the job, but that didn't mean much. She still had her own life to lead, and she didn't need to be grateful. She would have gotten the job one way or another.

Besides, Hannah had started this war when she'd upstaged her in front of Doreen. Nobody did that to her. Hannah was crafty, but not crafty enough—she was trying to play both sides, but she'd fail. She was probably getting a hefty fee for this little deception. She couldn't blame her; money was everything. Camille thought of blackmailing Hannah, but that could get complicated and she didn't like complications. Her allegiance was to Amal alone because he was the true power, and a wounded man was easier to manipulate. She didn't plan on being a nanny forever, but the role might come close to an end sooner than she'd thought. She'd get rid of Hannah, and Amal would pay her well to stay by his side because he'd feel she was the only woman he could trust. She grinned. Yes, Amal needed to know about Hannah's deceit, and she would be the one to tell him.

Chapter 17

Amal looked at the table settings. Tonight was an important night for him. For them. He had changed his image and lifestyle with Hannah's help, and he wanted to keep it going. She'd fit into his life better than he'd hoped. She even welcomed his son, taking him to bonding classes each week. That's why he knew they both needed to take their relationship to the next level. He'd ask her to move in.

Hannah came into the dining room and saw the decorated table. "What's this?"

"Sit down."

She did, curious. "What's the occasion?"

"I know I should wait until after dinner, but I can't." He handed her two pictures of houses.

"What is this?"

"I thought we should look into buying a house."

"We?"

"Yes, I'd like us to live together."

Before she could reply, Camille came in. "Oh, how are the Walkers?" she said to Hannah.

Hannah felt her blood turn cold. "What?"

"How would she know about the Walkers?" Amal asked.

Camille touched her chest. "Oh, haven't you told him yet?"

"Told me what?"

"I'll tell him later," Hannah said.

Camille ignored her. "Hannah hasn't been going to 'Mommy and Baby' classes. She's been taking J.R. to see the Walkers."

"No, she hasn't," Amal said. "Tell her, Hannah."

"She's right," Hannah said in a soft voice. "But I can explain."

"What's there to explain?" Amal said, outraged. "You went behind my back to my enemy and gave her my son."

"I just let her see him."

"Without my permission."

"For months," Camille added with glee.

"What's all this shouting about?" Doreen asked, coming out of her room.

"Go back to bed, Mom."

"You'll wake the baby."

"I said go back to bed!"

Tears filled his mother's eyes. "I just—"

"Don't shout at her," Hannah said. "You're angry at me. Not her."

Amal glared at her. "How I talk to my mother and what tone I use is none of your business."

"She's always sticking her nose in other people's business," Camille said.

Hannah pointed at her. "That's not your place—"

"She works for me and she's right," Amal interrupted. "What made you think you could get away with this?"

Hannah stood. "Let's talk about this in private."

Amal pounded the table with his fist. "We'll talk about it now."

Hannah sighed. "She was ill and—"

"I don't care if she was on her damn deathbed. She tried to destroy me. Did she pay you?"

"No. But I learned some things you should know."

"I know all that I need to. That you betrayed me."

"I thought that it would be good for J.R. to know his mother's family, and I wanted you to know that Jade—"

"He's *my* son, not yours. It's not your place to make decisions like that."

His words hit hard and deep. Hannah blinked back tears; she wouldn't cry. "You're right. He's your son, and this is your life." She pointed to Doreen. "She is your mother." She pointed at Camille. "And she is your nanny. And my opinions about any of them don't matter because I don't."

"I didn't—"

"Yes, you did, and you just proved it. As long as I follow your rules it's okay. But I'm not a possession who does what you tell her to and makes you feel needed. I went there because I wanted more for you and J.R. I wanted you to know how much Jade loved you so that you wouldn't feel guilty. I wanted to find out the truth for you, but now I realize that doesn't matter. Go on and hate. Hate that Jade died without telling you about your son. That your father left you without a reason. You can keep all that misery and pretend it's not there, but I won't live that way."

Hannah walked over to Camille. "And you, sweetie, may think this is a victory, but you've caused more damage than you could ever know."

Camille grinned. "At least I'll be around to pick up the pieces."

"Don't get cut. The pieces are pretty sharp and hard to fix."

Hannah marched to the door.

"If you walk out that door…" Amal warned.

She turned to him. "Consider me already gone."

The moment Hannah left, Camille wisely disappeared into another room while Amal stood staring at the closed door.

"Go after her," Doreen demanded.

"No," Amal said, taking the framed pictures of Hannah and himself off the fireplace mantel.

Doreen grabbed them from him. "You can't lose her."

"You heard her. She's already gone."

"You and your damn temper. Why didn't you just listen?"

"Because I didn't want to hear excuses."

"You said hurtful things—"

"And I meant every word."

"Just like your father."

"Don't pull that with me," he warned.

"He also said whatever he wanted to. He didn't care who he hurt, and neither do you."

"She betrayed me."

"And you didn't ask why."

"I don't care why."

"I'm ashamed of you. Do you think she doesn't know what you've been through? Wasn't she the one who helped you find your son in the first place? Wasn't she the one who stood by you during the Walkers' smear campaign? Wasn't she by your side in the courtroom, and when you went and bought things to prepare for J.R. to come home? Didn't she do all that for you? And now you're willing to toss her away?"

Amal briefly shut his eyes, struggling to keep from shouting. "She took my son to the Walkers—"

"Do you honestly think Hannah would do anything to hurt you? She's a bigger person than both of us, because she's thinking not of you or me but of J.R. She's making sure that you won't do to the Walkers what they'd done to you. One day your son is going to ask about his mother and her family. Are you going to continue the hate between you and them?"

"I—"

"You didn't even give her a chance to explain because you're too busy seeing your needs, your hurts, your pain. You shamed her in front of the staff. You treated Camille with more respect than Hannah."

"At least I know I can trust her."

"Right, you're the only one who counts. No one else matters as long as things go your way. You're unyielding, but that will have to change—maybe not for Hannah, but for J.R. You're a father now and you need to think beyond yourself, and if J.R. makes a mistake you can't just walk away."

"I never would. Haven't I thought about you? Haven't I provided for you and J.R.?"

"Always on your terms. What happens when or if

J.R. fights back? What if he sneaks into a movie you told him not to? What if he tells a lie and you catch him? What if he breaks something that means a lot to you?"

Amal shook his head. "I'm going to stay with him. I'd never disappoint him. I'm going to be a good father."

"Then you should try to be a good man first."

Hannah didn't cry when she reached home, which surprised her. She felt amazingly liberated. She no longer had to keep the secret. Her meetings with the Walkers had been weighing her down. She would have to tell Martha about Amal, and they would have to work it out on their own. She would no longer be the go-between. She could imagine the position poor Jade found herself in—caught between two strong personalities, too stubborn to back down from their stance. She had to give it to Camille—she had caught her. She should have stuck with her first instinct and not hired any of the nanny candidates.

But no regrets. She was sick of living with regrets and guilt. She'd seen what it had done to Martha. She wouldn't let it eat her up, too. She'd felt sad that her mother didn't like Amal, and that Amal didn't like Martha, and that her sister didn't like him or her. But that was all done. She wouldn't be a slave to people's opinions of her, because they always changed. She'd miss J.R., but he was too young to remember her. For the first time in her life she would live for herself.

For the next several weeks Hannah did just that. She dined with Dana and Natasha and was able to afford the high prices at the restaurants they chose. After uncovering the hidden Walker child and getting Amal's inventory back, she'd restructured her business to focus on independent research for small law firms and seen her clientele double. She treated Dana to a pair of designer shoes when she announced she'd gotten a promotion at her job and helped prepare a fabulous baby shower when Natasha announced she was expecting.

Then one day Bonnie came into the office with an engagement ring on her finger.

"It's beautiful," Hannah said as she congratulated her.

Bonnie beamed. "I was so shocked when he asked me."

"I'm really happy for you."

"I knew you would be. I just wish—"

Hannah shook her head. "This is a perfect moment. There's nothing to wish for."

"I want you to be my maid of honor."

"Of course."

Bonnie hesitated. "There's just one hitch."

"What?"

"Hector wants Amal to be his best man."

"That's fine," Hannah said.

"Are you sure?"

"I'm positive. I've no problem being civil to Amal, but Hector may have a problem convincing him."

Hector didn't have a problem at first telling Amal about his upcoming wedding and wanting him to be the best man—until he mentioned Hannah.

"She'll be there?" he asked as they played tennis.

"Yes, as maid of honor."

"What?"

"She's Bonnie's best friend."

"Can't she get another best friend?"

Hector cleared his throat and tried another strategy. "Hannah said she doesn't mind seeing you, but if you—"

"She said that?"

"Yes."

"Then it's fine. I don't care about seeing her."

Hector bit back a grin of triumph. "Thanks, man."

It was green. She hated the color green, but Bonnie loved it so Hannah would have to wear it. It had been a harrowing week. She had successfully organized and bought a gift for Natasha's baby shower, attended the fitting of Bonnie's bridesmaid dresses and went to an office party with Dana. Her friends' lives were on track while hers felt slightly derailed, but she was too happy for them to think of her own problems. She was carrying her dreaded maid of honor dress to her apartment, looking for the winter chill to completely welcome the coming spring, when a man blocked her path. She looked up at Peter and shook her head. "Not today."

"Even if I said 'please'?"

Hannah held up her dress. "Do you see this?"

He winced. "Do I have to?"

"It's my dress for a friend's wedding. I have a lot on my mind, and I'm not dealing with the Walkers anymore."

"I'm not here about the Walkers."

Hannah draped the dress over her arm. "Then what do you want? Want to come as my date?" she teased.

"Sounds like a good idea."

Hannah paused. "Are you serious?"

He smiled and his handsome face lit up in an astounding way. "I thought it'd be nice to have coffee sometime."

"You should smile more."

"It's not part of my job. So what do you say?"

"I never say no to free coffee."

Hannah enjoyed Peter's company more than she thought she would. He had a keen mind and a dry, droll humor that impressed her. He was the kind of man who could help her forget the man who still haunted her dreams each night.

She looked great; she looked carefree. Worst of all she looked happy. She wasn't supposed to look so happy and carefree. Not without him. Amal watched Hannah sitting in the café at a table with another man.

"He's a good-looking guy," Doreen noticed. "Even better-looking than you."

"He works for the Walkers."

Doreen ignored his sour tone. "Hannah has got herself quite a catch. He's single, without kids and great to look at. Serves you right."

Amal sipped his drink. He'd enjoyed these meetings with his mother. She appreciated the attention, and he had to admit that he didn't worry about her as much as he used to. Usually he liked hearing her opinion— although not today.

"Did you expect her to be like Evie and Jade and pine her life away for you? Did you expect her to lock herself away and never see another man because her heart belonged to you?"

Yes and *yes*, but he'd never admit it. But what right did Hannah have to be so happy when he was so miserable? She was the one who'd lied to him, betrayed him, and he had a right to be angry. When she'd left that night he didn't think she meant it. He'd anticipated a tearful apology the next day but got silence instead. "I have no regrets."

"No, of course not. That's why you haven't slept well in weeks—and don't blame J.R., because he's not the cause."

"I have a lot on my mind."

"Like how to win her back?"

"I don't want her back."

"No. It's just you and J.R. and that creature now. I'd warned Hannah about her."

"I trust her."

"Naturally, she's perfect. Although I always wonder why it took her so many weeks to tell you about what Hannah was up to."

"She said she didn't know if she should. She was trying to protect me."

Doreen groaned. "Are you really that gullible?"

"I believe her." Amal gripped his hand when he saw the other man lean toward Hannah and whisper something in her ear that made her laugh. No, he didn't want her back, but he could say hello since their friends were getting married. He could show how disinterested he was. He stood and walked over to their table.

"So, did you get an invitation?" Amal asked.

"Yes," Hannah said, looking up at him in surprise. "I'm the maid of honor."

"I'm the best man."

"I'm amazed anyone could convince you to walk down the aisle," Peter said as he looked up at Amal.

Hannah laughed. "As long as he's not making any vows, he's okay."

Amal's jaw twitched. "I need to talk to you."

Hannah pulled out a chair and patted the seat. "Go ahead."

"Alone."

"Peter and I don't have any secrets. How's Camille? I know you have no secrets with her, either." Hannah looked past him. "Where is she? I should say hello."

"She's home with J.R."

"Of course. It must be so nice to have someone you can really trust."

Amal sat and turned to Peter. "Will you excuse us?"

"No," he said and then continued sipping his drink.

"Yes," Hannah said, seeming to enjoy his unease. "Peter knew all about me trying to find a way to heal your rift with the Walkers. He knows all about how I was bribed by them and refused. He knows all about how much I tried to get Martha to see you. He also knows how you feel about me."

"I warned her not to do it," Peter said. "Everyone knows about your temper."

"You don't know anything about me," Amal said.

"Sure I do," Peter said in a low voice. "Why do you think I'm here enjoying what you threw away?"

Amal's eyes darkened. "Not for long."

Peter only smiled. "I know you won't live like a priest, so don't expect her to live like a nun."

Amal grabbed Peter's shirt and shot to his feet. Hannah squeezed between them. "Stop this."

"That temper's not helping you win any favors," Peter said.

"That's enough," Hannah said. "Amal, let him go."

Amal shoved him back down and Peter straightened his shirt.

Amal glared at her. "Hannah—"

"Let's not play games. I know that this is about pride for you. I left, and no one leaves you. So if you walk away you can tell yourself that you left me because it was your choice. You didn't hear a word I had to say— you didn't care. You locked me out. You claimed your son and your life and completely shut me out of it. I'm not going to beg or plead for you to take me back. I'm not going to ask for your forgiveness. You wouldn't accept it anyway. I finally realized that I don't need you to make me happy. I can be happy on my own, especially when I stop trying to please everyone else."

"I was going to ask you to live with me."

"And I would have said no, because I wanted to marry you instead." She stood, grabbed her purse and left.

Peter lazily rose to his feet. "She still loves you and you have no idea what she's done for you." He pushed past Amal and said in a low voice, "You don't deserve her, and I'm not sure you ever will."

Chapter 18

You don't deserve her. What did he mean by that? Amal thought with fury as he pedaled a stationary bike at the gym. He'd just completed a two-mile swim, but he couldn't rid himself of his last meeting with Hannah or forget Peter's words. What did the bastard mean that he'd never deserve her? He'd treated Hannah well. He cared about her. He was going to buy them a house and have her live with him. He'd fixed her parents' house. He was Amal Harper. He was a catch. Women wanted to be with him. After Hannah had left, he'd proved it. He'd gone on dates with a few different women for the past two weeks because he could and because he wanted to. It was early spring and he was feeling frisky, and he forced himself to enjoy every minute—although he was finding it difficult.

"You know you're taking a risk," Hector said in the office the day after one of Amal's nights outs.

"I'm just being social. I'm not doing anything more."

"But you have to be more careful with your image."

"Let me worry about my image. I passed my six-month trial period. Relax."

"But Hannah—"

"Hannah's not here."

"I'm just saying she helped you get J.R. Don't jeopardize losing him because you're angry at her."

But he was angry. Angry that she'd left him. Angry that she'd gone out with another man and didn't seem to miss him as much as he did her. She was the one who betrayed him. Why didn't anyone see that? Why was everyone on her side?

Amal drove home, wishing he could turn back the clock and make everything the way it was. When he entered the living room, he saw Camille playing with J.R. At least she was on his side. His son looked up at him and smiled and spread his arms wide. Amal knew he wanted to play the game he'd played with Hannah and the one his mother had continued, but it was too painful for him to try. Instead, he tickled him and then studied Camille. His mother's words echoed in his mind. Why had Camille waited so long to tell him about Hannah if she knew it was important to him? Her excuse of trying to protect him appeared flimsy now. He sat.

"Camille, what do you want?"

She looked at him, startled. "What do you mean, Amal?"

"Why didn't you tell me about Hannah sooner?"

"You're tired. Let me get you something to drink."

"I'm not tired."

"I told you that I was conflicted. I didn't know what to do."

"So you chose the day that I was going to ask her to live with me to tell me?"

Camille widened her eyes. "I didn't know you were going to do that."

"No, but you could have told me anytime before that moment. You could have come to my office, met me at the gym, called me, but you didn't. You waited for your chance to cause the most damage." He smiled without humor, remembering Hannah telling Camille about all the damage she'd cause. He'd been too blind and angry to register the weight of her words. Now he did. He nodded, reluctantly impressed. "Good job."

Camille sat on the couch beside him and touched his hand. "I wanted you to see who she really was before you made a mistake."

Amal pulled his hand away. "I already made one. Pack your things."

"Amal—"

He glanced at his watch. "If you want a reference, you'll keep your mouth shut, and you'll start now."

Amal picked J.R. up and went to his bedroom. He sat on his bed with J.R. on his lap. His son was the key. He needed to understand why Hannah had gone to the Walkers. What was their pull? He needed to know what the Walkers had said to persuade Hannah to do what she'd done.

As Amal walked up the circular pathway to the Walkers' mansion, he remembered the many times he had visited before.

"So you came to your senses?" Peter said, opening the door to Amal.

"Keep talking and I might lose it and take a few of your teeth instead."

"Just try. I saw Hannah yesterday. Took her dancing and enjoyed every minute of it."

"Did you bring J.R.?" Martha asked, coming to the door before Amal could reply to Peter.

Amal rubbed his fist, wishing he could connect it with Peter's face. "No."

"Oh," she said, disappointed, and then she recovered and led him to the sunroom.

Amal followed, remembering the times he'd come to dinner with Jade. He used to feel welcomed, but now he was an outsider.

"I was surprised by your request," Martha said once they were seated.

"Me, too, but I have to know what you and Hannah talked about."

"Mostly about Jade."

"Jade?"

"Yes. She didn't tell you?"

I didn't give her a chance. "No."

"She wanted us to be one big, happy family. I knew you'd never forgive me, but she was certain she could work on you. She was taking pictures of us and thinking of showing you a collage so that you'd approve of what she was doing. I can see that didn't happen."

"No."

"I am sorry for all that I've done. I know it won't make up for anything. But these words come from the heart. I kept you and James apart when I shouldn't have."

"How can I trust you?"

Martha looked down at her hands. "I don't know," she

said, helpless. She lifted her gaze. "But I've changed. Truly. I didn't realize how much until Hannah came with J.R. She forced me to see myself, and I didn't like what I'd become. Over these past several months I've worked hard to change. I know Hannah did the same for you."

"What do you mean?"

She smiled. "You're not the same man who dated my Jade. I know you loved her and I know you wanted to save her, but the love you had also drained you. When you used to come by I saw the strain on your face. When I saw you in the courtroom with Hannah, I knew you were tense, I knew you were worried. But there was a strength I'd never seen before, and that was because she was by your side." Martha shook her head. "My daughter was like a jewel that needed to be guarded and protected. She was beautiful to have, but at times her presence was cold comfort."

Amal glanced away, not wanting to admit the truth of her words. Jade had been so special to him, he didn't want to see her in any other light than as he remembered. He wanted to remember her talent for choosing an art piece, laughing with a gallery owner, posing for a picture with a bright smile. "She had her flaws, but don't we all?" he said.

Martha twisted the wedding ring on her finger. "Yes, and I'm willing to admit it. I wanted to call you, but I didn't have the courage." She rested her hands on her lap. "I do now. Whatever you want me to do, I'll do. Whatever you want me to say, I'll say. I'll do whatever I need to in order to make things right between us."

It was a bold statement, and he knew it was hard for her to say. It was even harder for him to accept. He wanted to hate this woman. He wanted to keep her at a distance and not see her again, but at the same time he sensed her sincerity and saw her solely as a mother who'd lost her child. He thought of losing J.R., and his heart twisted. They shared pain; they shared regrets. She had changed and so had he. Their future didn't have to reflect their past. Amal folded his arms, ready to negotiate. "I can bring him to see you, but it won't be weekly."

"That's fine. It's a start." Martha sat back, suddenly looking more relaxed. "Jade would have liked Hannah."

"They're nothing alike."

"I know, but I don't think she'd mind her raising her son."

Amal sent her a sharp look. "But she's not going to."

"And whose fault is that?"

He stood. "None of your business."

"I didn't take you for being a coward."

He sat down again and stared at her in shock. "A coward?"

"Why are you holding Hannah to a higher level than Jade?"

Amal shook his head. "She betrayed—"

"I know what she did, but I also know that my Jade did worse. I know that sometimes inventory disappeared that you had to cover for, and there was that artist in Spain—"

"I don't want to talk about that," Amal cut in.

"I know you weren't sure J.R. was yours because you know she wasn't always faithful, both in business and in your personal life. I know she hurt you. You excused her because of her addiction, but she had a selfish side that we both must admit to. So why are you so quick to forgive Jade and not Hannah?"

"Jade needed help. She was different."

"Yes, with Jade you could be a fun, carefree boy. You had lots of fun together, and you could relish in how much she needed you. But Hannah doesn't need a boy who can take her out dancing or sailing or to the many activities you did with Jade and the other women you chose. With her you have to be a man. So I guess it was good you broke up with Hannah, because you're not the man for her."

You don't deserve her. You need to be a good man. You're not the man for her. Amal drove home from Martha's house, all the words people had said to him over the past weeks swirling in his mind. Why did everyone think he wasn't the right man? Wasn't he a good man? Why did they think he fell short? Amal saw an attractive woman strolling down the street wearing a tube top and miniskirt and thought of Hector's concern about his partying. His friend was right. He was angry. But instead of facing Hannah, he'd behaved like a child and gone out doing everything that could have jeopardized his custody of J.R.

Amal thought of his reckless behavior as he tossed his keys on the foyer and walked to his mother's suite. She was out with J.R., and he knew he could trust her with him. He'd get a new nanny soon, but he wasn't ready for that yet. He sat in his mother's bedroom and glanced around, realizing that his past behavior had been as childish as hers when she used one of her episodes to get his attention. He had to admit that part of him hoped to get in trouble so that Hannah would have to come and fix things for him. At least then he'd have her attention. But he wouldn't do that anymore.

Amal stood and walked over to the picture he hated to face—the one of him and his father at a barbecue. He picked up the photo and studied it. Yes, he resembled his handsome father and he had his temper, but that's where the similarities would end. He wasn't going to disappoint those who loved him or walk out on anyone who needed him. He was a changed man. He didn't need Hannah to fix things for him, to help him, to support him or to guide him. He was ready to be there for her. To be someone she could depend on. He'd own up to his mistakes and take the steps he needed to be the man she deserved.

Hannah hummed as she flipped through her mail, thinking of the dancing spot where Peter had taken her. She was really starting to like him and wished she could make it more. But for now she would accept it for what it was—a chance to keep her from thinking about Amal, J.R. and Doreen. She shook her head. She had to accept that it was over. He'd gone on with his life, and so would she. Just as Hannah was about to toss her envelopes away as junk mail, she stopped and groaned when an invitation caught her eye. It looked harmless, but she was sure it would cause lots of drama.

Chapter 19

"Jacob's getting married," her mother wailed. "To the Yeles' daughter!"

Hannah stared at her mother from across the family room, remembering the phone call she'd received from her sister telling her that she'd caused trouble again. Right now her sister sat diagonal from her, smiling as if enjoying a gory horror movie. "She's a good person," Hannah said, recalling the fresh-faced woman her mother referred to. "I'm happy for him."

"Happy? How can you be happy when one friend is getting married and another is having a baby and you're..." She let her words fade.

"I'm what?"

"You're not. You missed a wonderful chance. Didn't I tell you not to waste your time with the American?"

"Yes."

"But did you listen? Jacob Omole was your greatest chance at happiness."

"No." Hannah leaned forward, ready to tell her mother the truth. "But there's something you should know." She glanced around the restructured room. "Let me tell you something about this house. When you and Dad were about to lose it because you couldn't make the repairs, do you know what Jacob did? He listened and then sent me chocolates. When Dad was in the hospital, he gave me flowers. When Dad first had his accident, he promised to stop by the hospital but never did. He bought me lunch instead. When I told him that your house couldn't be insured, he didn't offer to help me find contractors. He didn't even offer to give me a loan to make the repairs. He did all the romantic things, but not one thing I needed him to do.

"But when I told the 'American,' he not only gave me the name of a contractor, but he was the one behind the repairs. He's the one who added the landscaping. He just wanted to help. Jacob was always flash and flowers, but he was never around to wipe my tears."

Her mother stared at her. "Amal had the house fixed?"

"Yes."

"Then why aren't you with him anymore?"

Hannah let her head drop, not wanting to argue about another subject. "It's a long story."

"I know that I wasn't as friendly as I could have been," her mother said. "If you need me to go by his house and drop off some food, I will. I noticed he liked my—"

"Please don't," Hannah said quickly.

Her mother stood. "I guess he wasn't so bad. I should thank him," she said, heading for the kitchen.

Hannah inwardly groaned, knowing she'd leave the house with something to deliver to Amal. He'd never get it. She looked at Abigail and then pulled out an envelope and handed it to her.

"What is it?" Abigail asked, suspicious.

"A ticket to Paris."

"Why?"

Hannah shrugged. "Why not?"

"You're just trying to show off because business is doing well."

"No, I thought you may not want to be around while Mom fusses about the Yele daughter getting married."

"I don't care." She handed Hannah the envelope. "I don't need to go anywhere."

Hannah folded her arms, not taking it. "Go ahead and enjoy yourself."

Abigail placed it on Hannah's lap. "When I'm ready to go, I'll pay for it myself," she said and then left the room.

Hannah shoved the envelope back into her purse, placing her hopes of a better relationship away as well, and then walked out onto the porch where her father sat.

"So will I ever see Amal again?" her father asked.

"I told you what happened," Hannah said, taking a seat. "It's over between us."

He nodded. "So how long are you going to punish him?"

"I'm not punishing anyone," Hannah said, surprised by her father's words.

"Then why didn't you just apologize?"

"He wouldn't let me explain."

"That wasn't my question. Why didn't you just apologize? What you did was wrong."

"I know, but I—"

"Hannah, all you had to say was 'I'm sorry.'"

"He shouted at me in front of his mother and that woman."

He frowned. "Woman?"

"The nanny."

"I'm not saying Amal should have done that, but still you were wrong."

"But I—"

"You're doing it again. You're too busy explaining yourself and not admitting that what you did was wrong."

"I was doing it because I thought it would help everyone."

Her father gently patted her hand. "I know your intentions were good. You're always the one who wants to help others. But this time you overstepped your bounds. You saw this situation from one perspective but never took a moment to see it from his point of view. He's a good man trying to get his bearings in his new role. He already feels insecure as a father, and you went behind his back and basically said you knew more than he did, that you knew what his son needed more than he did."

Hannah threw up her hands. "You don't need to remind me whose son J.R. is. I know he's not mine. Amal made that very clear."

Mr. Olaniyi shook his head. "Don't misunderstand him. His words were just to hurt you because you hurt him. But I know he wants you to think of J.R. as your own. You are as much to blame for your breakup as he is. He had a right to be angry at you, and he had a right to not want to listen to your excuses at that time. And if you were more mature you would have let him cool down and then talked to him. You talk about his temper, but you have your own and you let it get the best of you." He folded his arms. "Consider yourself lucky he never asked you to marry him."

Hannah turned to him. "What do you mean?"

"You both would have failed."

"You don't know that."

"Yes, I do," he said with a knowing smile. "Because you both reached a point where unsuccessful marriages eventually head. The point where the union between you matters more than the individuals in the union."

Hannah rolled her eyes. "Have you been reading your citizen books again about the State of the Union?"

"Joke all you want, but I'm telling you what you need to learn if you ever plan to marry. You shouldn't have left. You should have stayed for J.R. and Amal—that is, if you cared enough. That's what a marriage is. You get over yourself and think of others. But your pride was hurt and his pride was hurt, and that's all you both thought about. So you're lucky you both found out now how unsuitable you are for each other."

"Unsuitable?" Hannah said, annoyed. "I would have made a great wife. I'm good for him. I can keep him focused, and I love his son and his mother. And Amal is good for me. He keeps me from being too serious, and when he's not flying off the handle he's considerate, funny, smart, determined, kind and— What's so funny?" Hannah asked when her father started to laugh.

"So how long are you going to punish him?"

Hannah let her shoulders drop, realizing how much

she'd revealed of her true feelings. "I can't go back to him."

"Too proud?"

She sighed. "Yes."

He shook his head. "It's not that."

"What?"

"You're just as afraid of marriage as he is because marriage isn't just about love. It's about compromise. You have to love each other enough to do that."

Hannah thought of her father's words as she and Amal walked down the aisle side by side during Hector and Bonnie's wedding. She did her best not to notice how good he looked, how wonderful he smelled and how much she missed him. Part of her wanted to admit how sorry she was, but another part of her wanted to scream at him for not seeing things from her side. But perhaps that was her trouble. It couldn't be all about her. Her father was right. She may have liked the idea of marriage, but she instinctively knew she wasn't ready for the realities of it.

The wedding was beautiful but long. The reception, which was held in the grand hall of a private club, was filled with relatives of both the bride and groom. There were lots of assorted food and pastries and plenty of dancing. Hannah spotted Doreen with J.R. over to the side but didn't have the courage to go up to them and say hello. She felt too vulnerable. Instead, she went outside and sat on a bench and stared up at the sky, which was a mixture of blue, pink and purple hues. The sound of laughter and music floated from the room behind her. It was a wonderful day and she'd survived it. She glanced down and saw some buttercups.

She walked and picked one up, remembering the time when a stranger arrived in her life and brought joy where there had been pain. She tossed the butter cup away. She could apologize, but she didn't think would change anything at this point. Too much time had passed and there was too much hurt between them. But it would be cowardly of her not to try. She picked up the buttercup again. She would try. She picked up another buttercup and another, thinking of presenting them to Doreen as a necklace. Just in fun. Maybe she could help her get close to Amal again. But she would be patient because he was worth the fight.

Hannah smiled to herself and reached for another buttercup when a black shoe came into view. She glanced up and saw Amal with J.R.'s stroller. She stood

"What are you doing?" he asked. "I know you could disappear in a garden bed, but I didn't expect you to try."

Hannah glanced down. She'd forgotten about her hideous green dress. "Don't make fun of it. I wore for my friend."

"What are you doing?"

"Just picking flowers."

"They look like weeds."

"You didn't think so the first time." She bent down and brushed one under J.R.'s chin. "Hey, cutie. Bet you don't remember me."

"He does," Amal said.

She stared at him, curious. "He's still young and it been months and—"

"He knows you because he sees your picture every day. At first I took all the pictures of you down, but then he told me not to."

Hannah's brows shot up. "He *told* you?"

"Yes, he doesn't talk yet, but we have a special father-son way we communicate."

"I see."

"Yes, he's taught me a lot of things. After scolding me for taking all your pictures down like a big baby, he told me to get a nanny who respected the people I cared about. No matter how well they treated him and me, J.R. thinks they should also treat others like Mom with respect, too."

"Smart little boy."

"Yes. He also said he doesn't like when I lose my temper and shout or get too stubborn." Amal shoved a hand in his pocket. "But mostly he taught me his favorite game. It's called 'Do you know how much I love you?'"

Hannah took a step back, tears springing to her eyes. "Don't—"

Amal took a step toward her. "Go on and ask me how much I love you."

Hannah shook her head, unable to speak.

He held out his arms to the side. "I love you more than this much, and I'm sorry I hurt you." He then let his arms fall. "I want you to be part of my life and I want you to be a part of J.R.'s life. Not because of my image, not because of my son, but because of me. I want to be in your life, and I want you to be in mine. And I won't lock you out of any part of it. I won't say it will be easy for me, but I'll work at it. I talked to the Walkers, and you were right about J.R. knowing the other part of his family. I never did. My father wasn't close to his family, and once he left they never tried to know me. I never faced how much it hurt. Damn, I'm babbling, and I don't babble." He took a deep breath. "What I'm trying to say is I want you to marry me and I want us to buy a house together and raise our son because that's how I want you to see him—together. So just tell me what I have to do to win you back."

Hannah brushed away her tears, grateful for this second chance and humbled that she hadn't lost him. "Forgive me."

He blinked and then frowned, confused. "For what?"

"I'm sorry I hurt you and I'm sorry I just walked out and let you be angry with me. I want you to forgive me for going to the Walkers behind your back and—"

Amal pulled her into the circle of his arms and squeezed. "I forgive you," he said, his voice muffled against her neck. "Don't cry. I hate to see you cry."

"Do you forgive me for everything?"

Amal tenderly brushed a tear away with his thumb. His voice shook with emotion. "For everything now and forever," he said and then claimed her lips with a passion that surprised them both. He crushed her to him as if afraid she'd leave him again if he let go. "Say you love me," he breathed.

"No."

Amal drew away and stared at her with a hint of fear in his eyes. "No?" he repeated just to make sure.

"No." Hannah wrapped her arms around his neck and smiled up at him, glad she was taking the chance to risk her heart. She felt an intense joy she didn't know was possible. "Because I plan to show you how much I love you for the rest of my life."

She picked J.R. up and kissed him on the cheek. "I missed you, little one."

J.R. giggled and hugged her.

Hannah hugged him back, and then she took Amal's hand. Together they walked back to the party, hand in hand toward their new life together. Amal was more than the man of her dreams. He was the man she wanted to make dreams with.

* * * * *